When Hearts Awaken

June Masters Bacher

HARVEST HOUSE PUBLISHERS

Eugene, Oregon 97402

Scripture quotations are taken from the King James Version of the Bible.

WHEN HEARTS AWAKEN

Copyright © 1987 by Harvest House Publishers
Eugene, Oregon 97402

ISBN 0-89081-610-7

Printed in the United States of America.

CONTENTS

. . . Now it is high time to awake out of sleep . . . The night is far spent, the day is at hand: let us therefore cast off the works of darkness, and let us put on the armour of light.
—Romans 13:11,12

To err is human; to forgive, divine.
—Alexander Pope

CHAPTER 1
Dilemma

Courtney Glamora sank into the great, black leather chair in the library, the envelope clutched to her heart. From the beginning she must have known that her wedding would not take place without incident. Too much had happened already. Trouble at the mines. The Bellevue Brothers popping in and out of her life and Clint's like jack-in-the-boxes. And then Clint's blindness. Most of all, the blindness.

And now this.

"I should have been warned by Lance's letter," she whispered now, looking at the ancestral lineup in the shadowy room. "But I am so prone to allow imagination to be my master. I didn't want it to seize the bit this time and go galloping off on a trail of mystery . . ."

Courtney paused and tried to remember exactly what her childhood sweetheart had written after returning to his Atlantic Seaboard home. She had made it clear that she was in love with Clint and expected to become Clint's wife and remain in the Northwest. Yes, Lance could write to her. And, yes, she would answer. But nothing would change her mind.

Dear Lance. How sweet he had been . . . writing of the sale of the family home, Waverly Manor . . . scraps of information of former acquaintances . . . and what little he knew of her mother.

It was the startling turn of events concerning her mother that troubled Courtney now. Mother had married a man of title and accompanied him to Europe where he promptly spent the Glamora mining fortune in riotous living. Now, for reasons unknown, she had left her older daughter, Vanessa, in London and returned to take a small cottage on the Eastern seashore.

The Lady Ana, Lance wrote, saw herself as delicate and felt that the "drowsy quiet" would restore her. And he sent Mother's address.

Arabella Kennedy sniffed at the news. "She made her bed."

Efraim, Courtney's brother, said he would be in touch immediately, see that their mother was taken care of financially, and Courtney was to go ahead with plans for the Christmas wedding. "Doesn't little sister know that the impatient bridegroom will never wait for her nineteenth birthday after all the postponements?" Efraim had asked.

But Courtney had written a note to her mother. And now (Courtney covered her face with her hands)—and now—Mother wanted her to come "home." The pitiful letter tore at Courtney's heart. Surely, Mother wrote, her youngest daughter knew that what "your father left me was infinitesimal, but dear John (that would be Sir John Ambrose, who never worked a day in his life, Efraim had told Courtney) had so little but a loving heart—in the beginning—"

They had each other, Courtney thought sadly. But, of course, that was not enough. The dashing Sir John managed to get everything signed over to him as Courtney remembered Efraim's account, and their mother was left in penury.

How long, the Lady Ana Bellevue Glamora Ambrose's letter wailed, could a woman of her breeding exist "with no new clothes . . . not even a knowledge of what is in fashion . . . hence, unable to be seen in fashionable society . . . that is, providing I were well enough physically and financially . . . ?"

Courtney did understand, did she not, that as a grown-up she should know that there had been no love between her parents? "I married Gabriel Glamora only because of parental pressure and, yes, his fortune. It seemed the thing to do. Now I realize that I should have remained at Waverly Manor after his death. As it is, I have lost all means of support—and my beloved family—"

The latter came as an afterthought, Courtney knew. The time was long past when she could think of her mother as loving anybody but herself. Her golden-goddess mother, whose love she coveted as a child, had fallen long ago from the pedestal on which her children had placed her. Efraim and Courtney, at least. And of course poor Donolar, whose infirmity made him unacceptable, had never known his mother. Courtney wondered fleetingly why he had never asked about Mother. She wondered, too, what had happened to Vanessa. Her older sister was no longer the toast of London, and Lance had mentioned Vanessa's fleeting love affair. But that she would allow Mother to travel across the ocean without her? Why was Vanessa still in London?

Courtney clutched the letter to her bosom and wept for them all. Things could have been so different if Mother had made a real home—the kind of Christian home God expects of people who enter into the sanctity of marriage. If only they could have lived on this side of the continent instead of the other. Here in Clint's "Dream Country" where perhaps two people met eons ago on Indian trails that crossed one another in a journey to the great waters of the Columbia. Where survival demanded that they become friends, nurturing that friendship into a godly thing which reached out to embrace all others as a fort was built and cabins sprang up around it. Where peoples of all languages survived wars, plagues, pestilence, and the cruelties of nature because they invoked God's blessing on their labors in the struggling little settlement. Love, that's what they had. And only now was Mother realizing she needed it. But her price would be Courtney's happiness.

Weary of thinking, Courtney made her way to the window to watch two fluffy clouds scudding across the sunset sky like two of "Mouser's" kittens afraid of losing their mother. The grounds below were patched with the first snowfall laced together with shadows from the deep forest beyond. An able-bodied breeze, soft as velvet, sprang up to bring the scent of Donolar's early-winter roses to mingle with the pines. Roses of Heaven, he named them, because of their late gift. The scarlet beauties would remain in bloom until after the wedding, Efraim's twin assured her, to mingle with the mistletoe and holly. The others could plan Courtney's dress and work on the reception, but Donolar would arrange the decorations. Too bad the butterflies would not be there to enjoy the magical moment, but he would share it all when they returned.

Dear, sweet Donolar. With his vivid imagination and his amazing grasp on the Bible and work of the poets. How was she going to leave him?

The last rays of the day's sun lit up the multipaned windows, set like a thousand eyes in the weather-worn roof. Courtney still marveled at the architecture of the strange house, its added-on ells and bays reflecting changing needs of its inhabitants from the earliest until the present ones: Cousin Bella, Courtney, Clint (when he could leave the mines), and—more recently—Efraim. Actually, there were more! There was Donolar who preferred his own quarters, a little cabin on his Isle of Innisfree. There were Mandy, the ebony-faced cook, and Mrs. Rueben, the sober German housekeeper. They were "family," too. And would one actually call Dr. George Washington Lovelace of "homeopathic medicine" and Brother Jim, who punched it out with Satan as he had with his contenders in the ring, *guests*? Even though they were at Mansion-in-the-Wild only for evening meals or when there was a physical or spiritual need, they were family. As was the whole Washington settlement, Courtney thought with a pang of premature homesickness.

"How can I leave them all, Lord?" Courtney whispered the prayer with dark eyes turned upward to a changing sky. Misty clouds, like spindrift, caught and clung to a half-dollar silver moon overhead and one by one the stars winked on.

She rose and stood before the ancestral portrait. Her troubled eyes met the uncertain pale ones of Grandfather Bellevue. For a moment, the eyes had lost their aristocratic stare. And surely she did not imagine the "I told you so" look in the glowering black eyes of Grandfather Glamora. No miner's son could hold onto a fickle, self-centered woman, they said. But it was her father, "Big Gabe"—the only adult who had ever loved her—to whom Courtney turned for comfort.

"Why, oh why, does Mother go on hurting us?" she whispered.

And there her conversation ended. From below came the muted sound of a horse's hoofs on the pine-needled trail.

Clint!

The house, the family, her mother—all of them— were but a closed album. Clint, the only man she could ever love, was home! She never remembered descending the stairs to be gathered in his arms. Words could wait.

CHAPTER 2
Commitment

One, two, three, four, five, *six!*

The appointed dinner hour of Arabella Kennedy, the mistress of Mansion-in-the-Wild. Like curfew, there were to be no violations.

Courtney, who had taken extreme care with dressing, counted the strokes of the grandfather clock. Counted them again as they echoed from room to room of the great house. Something in their chime warned that time was running out—some inner sense that whispered to her heart. She must reach a decision this night . . . but how?

At the door of the candlelit dining room, dark eyes searching for Efraim, the girl was unaware of the picture she made and that Clint was regarding her tenderly, his deep-blue eyes saying she was something that stepped from last night's dream. Since regaining his eyesight, Clint drank in her special kind of beauty as if his thirst would never be quenched. The blue-black hair, so demurely parted in the center, and sweeping over her ivory cheeks—so severe and yet begging to be rumpled by his chin. The perfect arch of her brows and the gold-tipped lashes that screened her dark eyes from his—almost as if she did not want to meet his gaze. Those eyes could sparkle with newfound gaiety since she came to this pioneer settlement. But tonight? Tonight, they were grave, as if mirroring her soul. *What's wrong, my darling?*

But Courtney did not see the tender concern in his eyes. In that tick-of-the-clock second that she hesitated, Courtney saw that Efraim was not present. Not that he was expected. But she needed him. She would have to consult him concerning their mother's plight. And perhaps Cousin Bella. Come to think of it, what she and Clint did would ultimately affect the loving group of relatives and friends assembled here. No, she was being illogical. Marriage was a private affair. First, she and Clint . . .

All eyes had turned toward her. With a graceful swish of her long yellow gown, she moved toward the chair Clint had pulled from the table for her. Donolar brought her a yellow rose to pin in her hair. Doc George seated Cousin Bella. Brother Jim seated himself. Mandy and Mrs. Rueben would remain standing until after the preacher's prayer. Then, after bringing the hot food from the kitchen they, too, would be seated.

Oh, how I love you all, Courtney's heart cried out as Brother Jim began his long incantation of praise. Clint took her small hand in his great, protective one and Courtney's heart soared upward to heaven where Brother Jim declared, in closing, they would all meet at the table of the Lord.

Courtney was unable to imagine a more wonderful group with whom to spend eternity. And yet, the lump in her throat would not allow her to join in the *Amens*.

She had never been good at making decisions. Mother had made them for her, the final one being to bundle her off to the Pacific Northwestern settlement to stay with a distant cousin whom Courtney, then 16, scarcely knew. Ah, but time had changed all that. In the two years Courtney Glamora had been among the settlers she had become a woman. A true pioneer. Capable of making her own decisions. Was it her mother's letter that took her back to the wavering uncertainty of yesteryears?

The conversation droned around her like the busy hum of bees when they found the ancient apple trees in blossom. But Courtney did not hear. It was as if she were that same lonely child, caught up in a whirlwind—wondering where she would land, or if she would land at all.

"*So!*" Brother Jim's deep voice boomed. "What do you say to that? If the date is acceptable—Clint? Courtney?"

Startled at the sound of her own name, Courtney jumped, then colored in embarrassment. "I—uh, whatever Clint says—"

Having no idea of what the question was about, she turned imploring eyes to Clint. The others, she saw from the corner of her eye, were smiling indulgently, having taken her embarrassment as a charming maidenly blush.

Clint covered beautifully. Oh, how she loved him!

"I would say," he repeated for her benefit, "that Christmas Eve would be absolutely ideal. But, having made no previous trips to the altar, I confess a certain amount of ignorance about such matters. I believe that it is up to the bride-to-be to name the date—and in private?"

The implied question was Courtney's cue. "Thank you all for caring," she said demurely. "A Christmas Eve wedding sounds beautiful—"

Only Clint noticed the sob that caught in her throat. The others mistook her words for an acceptance and began babbling excitedly.

Clint raised a silencing hand. "Whoa!" he laughed. "We beg for a moment of privacy before the grand celebration. If you will excuse us—"

And Courtney felt herself pulled to her feet gently and propelled toward the door. "The great escape artist—that's me!" Clint whispered in her ear.

She managed a wooden smile as he slipped his jacket over her shoulders and opened the front door.

"Clint—it's winter!" she protested as they stepped outside.

"So—we have a winter walk. If you shiver once—just *once*—I shall hold you like this!"

Strong arms encircled her and his chin rested on the part in her hair. Courtney felt warm. Protected. In love!

Night had set a million jewels a-twinkle in the deep-purple heavens. The great firs whispered a December song to the lovers below. Clint held her tightly in the circle of his arms. If only the moment could go on forever. But moments melt into minutes and time was moving on.

"Now," he said at last, "are you going to tell me what this is all about—and don't be coy with me, young lady. Don't you know I can read your mind?"

Clint leaned down and pressed his lips to the back of her neck. Courtney drew back. "Don't do that—please, Clint, you know I can't think—"

"That's the general idea," he whispered huskily as he drew her close again.

All defenses fled. And Courtney sobbed out the whole story. Mother was penniless. Mother needed her. Mother—

"Oh, Clint, am I not supposed to honor my father and my mother?" she ended pleadingly.

"Oh, my suffering darling. Of course, you are. And you have—all your life. But what does the Bible say about your duty to your husband . . . 'forsaking all others'?"

"But—but you're not my husband yet."

"I'm going to be! Now, you listen to me, my sweetheart. The question at hand is not *whether* we are to be married—it's *when*! We're supposed to be setting the date. If your mother is that penniless, how did she rent a cottage? And, as for looking after her—we will *both* go if necessary. *After we are married.* Now when will you marry me? Christmas Eve?"

Courtney's Christmas-bell laugh was his answer.

CHAPTER 3
No Second Thoughts

In her bedroom Courtney crouched by the open window, gulping in deep lungfuls of clean, sweet air. The outside world was filled with midnight magic and the scent of frosty evergreens. The rush of the wind in their branches set them dancing in a dark ballet, keeping time to the twinkling stars and the music in her heart. The broken-dollar moon had sunk. There was no light—except for a splinter that crept from between the drapes of Clint's room far down the upstairs ell. Was he, like herself, too excited to sleep? Or was it possible that he was having second thoughts?

Stop it, Courtney told herself sternly. *Stop reading other people's actions into your own, making your thoughts theirs. Stop allowing the insecurities of childhood to hold sway over the present.*

But that was the key, of course. The letter from Mother. Had she been too impetuous last night? So in love with Clint, so eager to be his wife, that she forgot the needs of a parent? She would feel better when she talked with Cousin Bella.

So thinking, Courtney prayed for guidance and "the peace that passeth all understanding" as she entered into the holy state of matrimony and dealt properly with her mother's dilemma. It was a relief to place her future in God's hands. Tomorrow . . . tomorrow . . . she would renew writing in her journal. "Dear God," she would write. "I just want You to know how happy You have made me. You have shown me what true love is these last few months. You must have known it would take some threat to Clint to deepen my love . . . and so You allowed his blindness to separate us briefly . . . but underneath our love was growing, strengthening like dormant bulbs beneath icy ground . . . bringing us both to realize how wonderful, how sacred marriage is . . . a union which is more than flesh . . . which lives and glows eternally in the soul . . . weathering all storms . . . all outside interference. Thank You . . ."

And then Courtney must have slept. Memories projected to walk hand-in-hand with dreams. She was in a dark closet, weeping bitterly for a father whose life had been snuffed out in the deadly cave-in at the Bellevue Coal Mines. Mother's beautiful face immobile behind the proper black veil but tapping a shapely foot behind the pew until the funeral service was over—leaving a child to grieve and the widow heiress to a fortune. *Oh, Mother, love me,—just love me*, the heart of Courtney cried.

The lonely years between faded out, except for fragments of recollection of her playmate, Lance, awkward in his efforts to comfort her and equally awkward in his advances as they entered adolescence together. And Efraim . . . coming home for brief vacations from law school. Efraim reassuring her . . . telling her that together one day they would leave this coast and explore the other. But Efraim was here and they must talk. She tried to reach out and touch him. But he faded like memories of Lance when he told her good-bye both times . . .

In their place stood Mother. "You remember Cousin Arabella (not waiting for an answer), you are 16 now and through finishing school, so a new experience will be good . . ." Flatly. Without expression. Without explanation. Without love.

And then Courtney was on the train with her governess. Heading into a "wilderness" to live with strangers.

What was this? A holdup? But who was the fearless stranger who faced the bandits so bravely? This oh-so-handsome man with sun-bronzed hair with its rebellious kink, clean-cut nose, and square jawline with its formidable strength . . . so lean . . . so lithe . . . and with the bluest eyes in the world. The stranger who saved her life. The stranger she was going to marry . . . spend the rest of her life with. Courtney reached out to hold onto the tail of time. But it had moved Clint away.

The scene was pushed out of her mind to make room for the vision of Arabella Kennedy. Dear Cousin Bella. Standing before her father's distant relative for the first time, Courtney had felt intimidated by the authoritative figure of Arabella Kennedy—her tall, somewhat angular, "dark side" kin, a study in black and white, including the dark braided hair with its sprinkling of gray. But her rich voice and carefully hidden tenderness soon won the young girl's heart. And how Cousin Bella loved her and Clint! "You must marry Clint now, my dear Courtney, before something else happens and the mansion falls into hands other than your own!" *What do you mean?*

But Cousin Bella, too, was swept away.

Courtney half-awakened when there was a sound in the hall. Then she drifted back to sleep to dream again. Only now the dream became a nightmare of memories.

She was back to the night of her arrival. Somewhere there was the hoot of an owl, followed by the lonely cry of a coyote. Then the strange woods were filled 'with a din of night creatures hooting, howling, and shrieking. The hoot of the owl drew closer to be joined with hordes of the frightening nocturnal birds . . . hooting . . . screeching . . . clawing at her door!

"Cousin Courtney . . . Cousin Courtney . . . so you are here to take what is rightfully ours! Who, *who*, WHO are you? Bring your *own* mother here. She will help. She is one of us!"

And then they were in her room. Great, feathered creatures, larger than herself. Their wings spread out. Four pairs of hideous, yellow eyes staring . . . daring!

But she did recognize them. The Bellevues—the two older ones (Hugh, wasn't that the name of Clint's half-brother who married Alexis?) and the other . . . but weren't they in jail . . . as was Milton, a younger brother . . . but what was Horace doing here? He was trusted by Clint . . .

But not completely by Cousin Bella, Courtney remembered in her terror. "Clint counts his blessings at having him at the mines during his blindness," Cousin Bella said of her nephew. "Me—I count the silverware!"

Secretly, Courtney had agreed.

"What do you want?" Courtney cried out weakly when at last she could find a voice.

"I dun brought you-all's breakfast, honey! I been a--knockin' fer a long time!"

Mandy! Dear, wonderful Mandy who brought the welcome combination of pancakes, daylight, and sanity.

*　*　*

After breakfast Courtney, thinking herself composed, put on a long black skirt and a frilly white blouse. Only a wide jade-green sash at the waistline broke the plainness. Her only jewelry was the opulent pearl, once belonging to Clint's grandmother, on her ring finger. Cousin Bella liked simplicity, and Courtney took pleasure in pleasing her.

"How lovely you look, my dear," Arabella Kennedy said as Courtney joined her in the sun room. "You are wise to be unadorned. Your face does wonders for any gown. A madonna-face, Clint calls it," she added without looking up, and busied herself pouring coffee for the two of them.

Courtney thanked her for the compliment and the coffee, then accepted the invitation to be seated. Did she sleep well after all the excitement? The question came while the older woman's eyes were still lowered discreetly.

"I—I—"

Courtney had not planned to mention the haunting dreams. But Cousin Bella, like her nephew, had a way of drawing secrets as magnets attracted metal. And Courtney found herself spinning out the entire dream.

"It has to mean something—something I can't put a finger on," Courtney finished with a little shudder.

"Drink your coffee while it's hot—good for the innards," Cousin Bella said practically. "Yes, dreams have meanings. They help us face and resolve problems. You have known all along that your mother was incapable of loving. Even at a distance, she would spoil your marriage to a miner! She bred these insecurities."

"My mother doesn't know. I—I haven't gotten around to writing her that. But I have this." The moment seemed right to share Mother's letter.

Arabella Kennedy accepted the perfumed sheet with no outward signs of surprise. She read it through silently and handed it back to Courtney.

"Clint knows?"

"Yes, I told him last night."

Cousin Bella stirred her coffee. "I am proud of you, sharing the inner courts of your heart. I only wish I had had the gumption when George Washington proposed. But let us keep to the subject. And I am proud of you and Clint for setting the date. Now, no more second thoughts! Here and now we will put the burden of the future on God's shoulders. They're broad!"

CHAPTER 4
A Letter to Mother

Having reached her decision, Courtney eagerly set to work on an ambitious letter to Ana Bellevue Glamora Ambrose. It was just as well that Clint would be unable to come home until after the dinner hour, Courtney told herself practically. At the same time, her heart yearned for him. Yearned desperately like an irresistible tide. Every moment away from him was a moment wasted. How could she have supposed for one irrational moment herself capable of postponing their wedding again? Never, *never*, NEVER!

So thinking, Courtney seated herself at the great mahogany desk in the library and drew out a sheet of Cousin Bella's blue stationery. And then she frowned. The words did not come easily. Praying for guidance, she picked up the pen, dipped it in the inkwell, and began— pausing often to pray again.

> My dear Mother:
> There is so much to say that I find words a poor tool. I beg you to try and understand my needs as I understand yours. First, let me express delight at receiving your letter. It is comforting to know that you are back in the place that is "home" to you but no longer that to me. I am saddened, of course, that you find yourself without means; but rest assured that Efraim and I will never allow you to suffer

further financial embarrassment. Efraim, I believe, has begun the process of having funds transferred to you. It will come from the earnings from his law practice established here and I will further it with the small allotment he found left to me to care for Donolar, whom we have grown to love so very much. . . . I am deeply remorseful that you are unhappy and unwell and it grieves me that I am unable to honor your request at this time. But I know that you will understand when I tell you that plans are underway here for my marriage to a Mr. Clinton Desmond, nephew of my late father's cousin, Arabella, to whom you sent me when you were to wed Sir John Ambrose . . .

Courtney paused, remembering. Should she say more or consider the matter closed? No, she decided, as she resumed, there was more to be said.

The man who has asked me to share the rest of his life is most wonderful. He has the qualities I have hoped to find in a mate. I find Clint generous to a fault, hardworking, gentle, and kind—a devout man, who will make an ideal husband and father. Together we will establish a Christian home which is time- and world-proof. That home, at least for the present, will be with Cousin Bella in her Mansion-in-the-Wild. It would take an entire letter to describe the enormous house (not at all like the wilderness houses you supposed the Washington Country to have); but, for now, suffice it to say that it is a place where love abides . . . and need I assure you that Clint and I adore one another?

Again Courtney laid down her pen. It would be futile and somewhat cruel to expand on the subject of the sanctity and purity of the love between her and Clint. Futile, because the Lady Ana had no understanding of such love or that it can be blessed by a far Greater Love. And cruel, because it would be like driving the harpoon in and giving it a twist to expand on the subject to a woman who had failed one man and been foiled by another. It was better to tell her mother what her delicate ears wished to hear. To make Clint acceptable in her sight. And then to reassure her concerning her own welfare, more important to her selfish heart.

She longed to describe the wonderland here and the kindred spirit existing among the settlers, but refrained. And Mother would think she had taken leave of her senses were she to describe Doc George, the loving Santa who dispensed pills instead of toys, or Brother Jim whose sermons were knockout blows that sent *Amens* echoing down the canyons. Best not tell her of the heirloom ring set with the lovely pearl either. Pearls were bad luck, Mother had declared of Courtney's father's gift. They were for tears. . . . Instead she wrote:

> As I told you, Clint is generous. He has promised that the two of us will come for a visit after the Christmas-Eve wedding. You will be interested to know that Clint has four half-brothers who are Bellevues, related on his mother's side to us—but distantly. (Why say more either good or bad about people Mother would never come to know?) Would that it were possible for you and Vanessa to be at the wedding. Do bless us from afar. I am sure that Cousin Bella, Efraim, and Donolar would wish to have me send you their regards.
>
> Love,
> Courtney

Courtney shuddered as she tried to imagine her mother's disdain at the news. But, determinedly, she sealed the blue envelope.

CHAPTER 5
The Question and
the Answer

The snow had disappeared by Sunday except for white patches lying in shadowy hollows of the hills. But the cold had strengthened, Courtney noted, as Clint tucked a lap robe about her legs before climbing into the carriage and seating himself beside her.

By edict of Cousin Bella, Clint and Courtney would occupy the carriage holding flowers for the morning worship service alone since they were betrothed. When Courtney, according to her stiffly correct upbringing, asked innocently if it would be proper, Arabella had sniffed so indignantly that the white ostrich plume on her black bonnet quivered.

"Stuff and nonsense! But to make it proper, my child, the rest of the family will follow you closely—never taking a watchful eye off of you, of course."

That had been over a year ago. And so much had happened. But the practice had not changed. Cousin Bella, regal as usual in her black suit set off by a silver cross pendant, rode up front with Donolar, who drove with practiced skill, in the second buggy. The backseat was occupied by Mrs. Rueben and Mandy (the German housekeeper having forgiven the cook—because it was the Sabbath, mind you!—for adding salt to her carefully prepared sauerkraut-and-sausage dish). Courtney smiled with renewed appreciation for the family which had come to mean so much to her here. Clint returned her smile and reached for her hand.

"I love you," he said.

Courtney's heart did a handspring. "And I love *you*—but, Clint, the others are watching—"

"My sweet little madonna," he whispered in appreciation but did not let go of her hand. "That reminds me, we will have little time alone after Brother Jim announces the date today, so on the way home I have something to ask you."

"You've already asked it!" She tried to make the words sound light, but the strange sense of foreboding—which persisted in being her shadow—was back. Why did she still feel that she was sitting atop a volcano which might erupt at any given moment?

They were entering the dense wood section, requiring Clint to let go of her hand. *But not for long, Lord!*

How still the world lay. So still that a snap of frost in the fir branches overhead echoed as if the tree might have been struck by a woodsman's ax. Courtney drew a deep breath of the bracing air and found it scented with evergreens from the box in back of their buggy. Donolar refused to part with a single rose until after the wedding. Cousin Bella said they would substitute the last of her rosy chrysanthemums that lingered in a shady corner of the fading garden. Donolar was delighted.

"We will mingle them with pine and balsam," he said, "and it will be like mixing Thanksgiving and Christmas!"

So now, ever so softly in his flute-like voice, he was singing the hymns of Thanksgiving praise and the sweet carols of Christmas as the two carriages neared the Church-in-the-Wildwood. " 'We gather together to ask the Lord's blessing' . . . 'How silently, how silently the wondrous gift is giv'n . . .' "

The gift of the silent forest. The gift of Donolar. The gift of love. How much Mother had missed . . .

The weathered little church with a spire that pierced the December sky loomed up suddenly. Larger inside than it looked outside, it was already crowded, Courtney knew, with people from miles around. Women who, as circumstances allowed, had exchanged their identical dresses with matching poke bonnets for a few Sunday items they found offered at the Company Store in an attempt to look like their beloved "Miz Courtney." Their men would appear in a variation of attire ranging from dated dark suits with stiffly starched collars to those in buckskins worn by the trappers or unlaundered garb of the miners. This she had come to expect. This she accepted.

But she could not feel comfortable with Horace Bellevue. Courtney was ashamed of her unfounded suspicions and wondered what evil spirit prompted her to be judgmental. But, even as conscience accused her, she found her eyes searching the woods as if the man lay in waiting instead of being inside with the other worshipers. She must purge herself of the wicked imp inside her . . . concentrate on the magic of this day . . . and come to accept Clint's half-brother as a part of her family.

With a carefully arranged smile, Courtney accepted Clint's hand and—holding her gray skirt just a fraction above her high-button kid shoes, stepped lightly to the ground. And then she frowned. Surely that nattily dressed man was Horace. He had melted into the crowd of new arrivals before she could be sure. And why on earth shouldn't he be here? Still—

"Why so pensive, little one?" Clint was busy tethering the team, but he had not missed her facial expression. The moment was saved by Donolar's voice urging Cousin Bella to allow him to assist her. And she consented. Time was when Arabella Kennedy would have been offended.

"Are you concerned about your aunt, Clint?" Courtney's concern was genuine, but it served to turn Clint's question aside, too.

"Yes," he said, joining Courtney to take her arm. "Watch out for the pinecones—you and those silly high heels! But

I think Aunt Bella will improve once we are married. She frets a lot—worrying about the mine—and us. She wants nothing to stand in the way of the wedding—"

"Nothing will!" Courtney promised as they stood aside for Donolar to lead Arabella Kennedy up the rough steps; and then the procession entered the crowded church.

Brother Jim was in fine form. Strutting to the rickety pulpit, which he refused to allow "abominated" by repair, the gorilla-like man paused before the expectant congregation. First with his hands in his pockets. Then with one of them loosening his too-tight collar and the other slicking back his hair which a ray of winter sun had turned to a burning bush. He had an important announcement to make, there could be no doubt. But first the admitted pugilist had a few rounds to go with Satan and his followers. After a long prayer, he doubled his great fists as if to deliver the knockout blow and castigated "sinners who're trying to crawl through the ropes of the ring to get into heaven by themselves!"

Satisfied with a chorus of Amens, Brother Jim mopped his sweating face with a red bandanna, then calmly tightened his collar. The big moment was at hand!

"Ladies and gentlemen," he said, dropping his voice so low that those on the back seats had to strain to hear, "it is my pleasure to announce that I will perform the ceremony which will unite our beloved brother, Clinton Desmond, to the woman God has given him to cherish, Miss Courtney Glamora, come Christmas Eve. And all are invited to serve as witnesses!"

The Reverend Brother lost his audience. Without awaiting the benediction, the congregation pushed forward to embrace Courtney and Clint. Courtney was sure she had never been so happy. Even the appearance of Horace Bellevue did not spoil the moment even though, she remembered later, he held her hand too long as the others waited.

At last they were on their way home. And this time when Clint reached for her hand, Courtney moved closer to him. "It's official now," she whispered.

"Yes," Clint said soberly, "it's official even though there remains a matter to be settled."

Courtney tensed. "Your question."

"How many children are we to have?"

"Oh, Clint," she gasped in relief, "is that all?"

" 'Is that all?' she asks—without naming the number."

Clint would never know the fears her mind had conjured. Or the flood of happiness which bathed her now. As a matter of fact, Courtney's mind had done a swing of its own. She was seeing a line of fat cherubs in pink and blue sleepers (all looking very much like their father) holding up the Bible and asking, "What makes the grass green, Daddy?" "How old is God?" "Tell us . . . it's all in here . . ."

"Well?" Clint squeezed her hand until it hurt.

"Twelve, I think," she said, remembering happily her talk with Cara. "Yes, a dozen sounds—"

"Just right!" And, disregarding the so-called "watchful eyes" of those behind them, Clint kissed the top of her head.

CHAPTER 6
Fair Exchange

In the whirl of activity following announcement of the wedding date, Courtney pushed all apprehension into the far closets of her heart. "I am ecstatic with happiness, Lord," she wrote in her journal. "I do believe that Donolar's Christmas roses will bloom just in time for the ceremony. Mrs. Rueben and Mandy are at a temporary truce and already baking jam cakes and sugar loaves for the feast—not that they'll be needed what with every homemaker in the valley bulging their pantries. Cousin Bella (bless her, Lord!) has a new lease on life it seems and is ordering everybody around as if she were a lady sergeant about to take the next hill—all this in preparation for seating at the reception. And, oh, the wedding dress—how lovely it is! How lovely the world . . . how lovely the relationship between Clint and me . . . how lovely, Lord, Your love!"

If Horace were a traitor, Clint would suspect. And Clint would help her and Efraim resolve her mother's problems—real or imagined. Nothing was going to spoil the joy of one Courtney Glamora!

It all seemed too good to be true. To reassure herself, Courtney went to the closet and removed the sheet which had protected her wedding dress during Clint's long convalescence. Surely, she thought as she caught her breath in admiration, she had forgotten how lovely it was. Elegant in its simplicity, the white silk mull skirt billowed out as if to emphasize the waistline, shirred to no more than the span of a man's hands. And oh, the waist! The tucks falling obediently into place to let the Valenciennes lace yoke and lace insertion on the three-quarter mutton-leg sleeves be the center of attraction. Cara Laughten had hemmed the gown by hand—and what was *this*? Why, Cara had added a dainty blue ruffle to the top petticoat. It peeped discreetly out as Courtney, with a singing heart, swirled the skirt about her legs. "Something blue"!

The "something old" was a number of things, Courtney reflected—counting the blessings that enfolded this household, really this entire valley! But more tangible was the priceless pearl on her finger. However, Cousin Bella had begged the question. And Courtney was only too happy to oblige. Tenderly, she removed the quaint lace cap which had belonged to her cousin, feeling tears gather in her eyes at the memory of how a couple, once in love like her and Clint, had let love, marriage, and children slip through their fingers. But she was glad to see that Arabella Kennedy had returned the seed pearls to their rightful place as trimming. Once she had called them "tiny tears" . . .

After putting the dress away, Courtney wrote to Lance thanking him for keeping an eye on her mother and asking that he continue to do so. She told him then of her wedding date. "I only wish that you could be here for the occasion," she said sincerely. "Remember, Lance, that you will always hold a special place in my heart."

Donolar was taking Cousin Bella to the fort for supplies later and she could post the letter. And while they were gone Courtney planned to accept Mandy's invitation to start cooking lessons. Sure, Mandy would remain with them, as Cousin Bella said, but Courtney felt a keen desire to be able to reach her husband's heart through his stomach *herself* if need be.

Mandy welcomed her with open arms. "Welcome, honey-babe. We's gonna start with pastry—rememberin' Mr. Clint's weakness fo' pies."

The kindly cook wrapped one of her own snowy aprons around Courtney's middle, then—with a mellow laugh——wrapped it again before tying it. "I do declar, sweet chile, y'all be needin' rich cookin' wors'n he do!"

Mandy then busied herself sifting flour from the bin. Once, twice, three times, she sifted. "Nex' add salt—jus' uh pinch, like so," and she lifted a plump, black hand to demonstrate how much lay between her thumb and forefinger.

"Do you mean you have no recipe?" Courtney asked in surprise. "I can never remember all this, so let me write it down for us."

The dark face clouded in despair. "Y'all know I can't be readin', don' you, Miz Courtney hon?"

It was Courtney's turn to be dismayed. "I'm sorry if I embarrassed you, Mandy," she said kindly. "Let me write down your instructions for myself. I've had absolutely no experience in the kitchen. I remember a *White House Cookbook* being in our kitchen one of the few times I was able to steal in there."

"Nothin' like soul food," Mandy said darkly. "Aw right, y'all put it on paper if it's pleasin'."

Courtney nodded. Then as Mandy busied herself with "double han'fuls," "hawg lawd size uv uh goose egg," and "leaven' like dis here," Courtney translated as best she could into cup-, tablespoon-, and teaspoonfuls—all the while thinking that she would offer to help Mandy learn to read.

"Now, we's gonna mix. An' nevah y'all be payin' no 'tention t'what them fine foks sez 'bout cuttin' with a knife. No siree, jus' git into it with yore han's, honey."

Mandy backed away. "Yore turn."

Courtney hesitated. "Me? I—I don't know—"

"Course you don'! And this'll larn y'all! Jus' don' let pie crust know yore 'fraid er it'll have th' bes' uv th' fight!"

Courtney slipped the pearl from her finger and felt for a pocket in the apron. Alas! One was completely in back, the other buried beneath the overlapped apron in front. Lifting the apron, she slipped the ring into the pocket of her blue-striped pinafore.

Half an hour later Courtney was wiping flour from her face and vainly trying to free her hands of the stuck-tight pastry. Mandy laughingly freed Courtney's hands and told her to wash up while the pastry chilled a spell in the springhouse. It would be just right, she said as she wrapped the ball of dough in cheesecloth, for baking a "goozeberry pie fo' suppah."

Courtney stripped off the soiled apron. "Mandy," she said as she wrestled with the knotted strings, "wouldn't you like to be able to read the Bible?"

"De good Lawd alone be knowin' how much!"

"Then let me teach you to read. It would be a fair exchange."

Mandy shook a curly-topped head. "I ain't able— nevah havin' no larnin' like white foks—"

"Nonsense! Mrs. Rueben is learning, so skin tone has nothing to do with it—just opportunity."

Mandy's great, brown eyes flashed, then rolled to show the whites dangerously. "Whut dat woman kin larn, I kin! When could y'all hep me?"

"Immediately! I'll label the measuring spoons—see S-P-O-O-N? Then cups, sifters—everything you'll be using. You can do it, Mandy. I know you can!"

"De Lawd gonna bless y'all, mah baby!" Great tears rolled down the ebony face.

"He already has—a million times over! And now, Mandy, I guess I will take a little walk before dinner."

She hugged Mandy and thanked her, but forgot to return the ring to her finger.

CHAPTER 7
Lost!

The air was brisk and the woods hummed an invitation as Courtney walked the trail she had walked so often before. Without conscious intention, she found herself picking her way to the spot so dear to her heart. It was on the cliff above the jubilant stream where she and Clint had shared a first picnic—and a first kiss. It was here, too, that Lance had painted his masterpiece, using Courtney as a subject. "Her Majesty" he had called it and the portrait had won the hearts of Eastern patrons of the arts.

"It now hangs in the New York Gallery," Lance had written, "making your face more famous than mine." Dear Lance. Ever the admirer. Ever the friend. Remembering his burning eyes in a face carved in stone the night she sent him back home to paint, Courtney knew that she was more than a friend to him. If only she could make him understand that there were different kinds of love . . . that her love for Clint was special.

Dreamily, Courtney seated herself on a mossy log above the wooded ravine and listened to the sibilant sounds of the stream below as it purled and rippled past shady shallows to join the mighty Columbia. If only she could paint like Lance . . . the mossy banks stained with the same deep green of the head-high ferns . . . the water dipped from the same dye pot as Clint's eyes.

It happened so suddenly. A feeling that she was being watched! Surely she had let the forest cast a hypnotic spell. This was a part of the Kennedy Estate. It belonged to Cousin Bella and was soon to be passed into Clint's hands. It was home. Why, then, the haunting sense of an unseen presence that made her look furtively over her shoulder?

She had failed to pin the little watch onto her bodice this morning, so she could only guess at the time as she glanced at the turquoise ring of sky visible overhead. It was streaked with a matrix of clouds lined with the pink of the slanting sun. She must get home. *Home*. The word sounded wonderful. Safe. Secure.

Even as she hurried down the crown of the hill, an icy chill tingled at her fingertips. She drew the woolen coat closer and forced her feet to pick up speed. But she must watch the trail, not fall. Forcing herself to remain calm, she dug her heels (Clint was right, they *were* too high!) into the moss and dried pine needles carpeting the trail.

Needing a bit of security, Courtney thrust her right hand into the pocket of her skirt in search of her engagement ring. It would be reassuring. But it was not there!

Frantic, she dug deeper. But the ring was gone. Desperately, she turned back into the woods which were slowly but surely turning from green to purple with early twilight. And then her imagination ran rampant. The forest looked actually spooky with gloom. She was being silly, she knew, to expect a monster from some childhood dream to leap from ambush. Even the rustlings beneath her feet had an uncanny sound. And was that an echo of each step . . . or was some creature stalking her? The blackberry brambles that tore at her pinafore became talons of the hooting owls that invaded her sleep. There was a hiss and the muted sound of leathery wings above her head. Bats!

But she *must* find the ring. Left out overnight, the pearl could be damaged. And, then, as Mother said, her wedding would begin in tears.

Purple dusk settled around her. The only light came from the tall fir trees reaching into the sky to garner one last russet ray of the setting sun which only they could see.

A night breeze whined in the canyon below and there was the distinct sound of rustling in the brush. No matter. She must slow down and pray that her eyes do the impossible—seek out and find the treasured heirloom. Search. *Search*. SEARCH!

And then, without warning, her foot struck a stone and she slipped . . . down, down, down . . . her flesh tearing and bruising and her mind conjuring up images of war-painted Indians. A coyote howled like some disembodied spirit. And then, battered and disoriented, Courtney found herself at the end of her fall. Ringless. And alone.

CHAPTER 8
Old Fears Renewed

Courtney lay stunned and still until the world righted itself. "Don't let me panic, Lord," she whispered as the sky, still palely pink with the sunset's afterglow, came into focus. She was lying on her back and, although her clothes were in shreds and her hands and arms were bleeding, she seemed no worse from the fall.

But that had been some tumble. And where on earth was she anyway? This was unknown territory. Not a part of the Kennedy Estate and, as she recalled, declared "off limits" by Clint and Donolar.

Forcing herself to stand, Courtney tried to get her bearings. But the small clearing was gathering as much darkness now as the woods on the trail far above her. The trail that she must somehow find a way to reach. Obviously, she would be unable to scale the cliff. Maybe another direction? She searched the gloom and sighted a stagnant pool behind her. And then, to her horror, she was facing the shutterless eyes of a building fallen to ruin in a tangled web of briars and thistles. A mill? The moss-clogged waterwheel suggested that possibility. No, it was a house—a large one that brought her uneasiness back. She must escape. And from what, she did not know.

Trying to control the fear tingling through her veins, Courtney looked around desperately. Her eyes came to rest on an ancient footbridge. But it led directly to the house. She shuddered, feeling her heart pick up momentum.

As if her fears were contagious, the bushes around her rustled, causing her nerves to go taut with tension. "Be calm," she whispered to herself to bolster her courage. Then, stiffening against fear, she plunged into a wooded area, not knowing where it would lead but feeling sure it lay in the direction of the Mansion.

And then she stopped dead still. There was a faint sound of footsteps. Somebody was—somebody *had* to be—crossing the bridge behind her. Stifling the impulse to scream, Courtney glanced quickly over her shoulder. And there it was! The faint outline—just a ghost, really—of a man! She wanted to run but could no more control her legs than one can break out of a dream. Instead, she stood in trance-like stillness, fear gripping her heart in a stranglehold. The sound on the bridge had stopped. That could only mean that the stalker was close behind—about to—

"You are wise to wait. Those woods would never get you home. Is this what you're looking for?"

Horace Bellevue!

Courtney did not know whether to be relieved or more frightened. In a sense, she was both.

Still unable to speak, she held out her hand to him, sure that he had found her ring. *How* made no difference. She was grateful, but seized by the urge to get away.

Horace's hand closed around hers as he handed her the ring. Courtney jerked her hand away. She should thank him; but instead, she was angry. Why was he spying on her when his brother, from whom he declared to be protecting her, was in jail?

"I found it by the log where you sat. I was here because—"

"I don't care *why* you were here!" Courtney spat out the words as she slipped the ring on her finger. "Just point the way back to the trail."

"In this darkness? Let me help you, Courtney. Don't you think I know the way—as much as I have been here?"

Courtney knew she had no choice but to accept his offer, yet was unable to resist saying, "Why do you always turn up where I am?"

Horace Bellevue answered question with question. "You don't like me much, do you, Courtney?"

"I don't understand you. *Please*—the trail!"

"This way," he said—and turned the opposite direction.

CHAPTER 9
Partial Explanation

To Courtney's surprise, there was a hacked-out passageway—like a route through a tangled jungle—that led back to the main trail. She could have vowed Horace Bellevue was leading her astray when he grabbed her arm roughly and steered her the opposite direction of Mansion-in-the-Wild. Should she apologize? No, he was still a question mark in her mind. What was he doing here?

"Don't look back," he cautioned once as they trudged upward. "This trail needs your attention."

Something in his voice made her suspicious. So suspicious that when they reached a little clearing where the trail doubled back, she glanced quickly over her shoulder, feeling a bit like Lot's wife must have felt.

Whatever she expected to see was not a ghostly light seeping from an upstairs window of the house she had thought deserted! The fear was back and, refusing any assistance from Clint's half-brother, she tore away from his grasp and ran as fast as her high heels would allow. Out of the woods at last, she saw the welcome lights of home. Now, if only she could slip in unnoticed—

"Courtney—*Courtney!*"

Clint stepped out of the shadows. Exhausted and sobbing, Courtney fell into his arms.

"Oh, my darling, what happened? Nobody knew where you had gone and I was starting out to search—*Courtney!*"

For the first time Clint had become aware that her dress was in shreds and she was wearing no coat. She must have dropped it in the fall or the climb back to the trail. Memory of the terrible ordeal had blurred some of the details.

"Here, take my coat. Oh sweetheart, you're hurt!" There was alarm in his voice as they stepped into a pool of light furnished by the brass lamp in the foyer. "Here," Clint's voice dropped to a whisper, "let me help you upstairs. I'll make your excuses at dinner—"

"No!" Courtney whispered back as they tiptoed up the stairs. "Just light a lamp—no, *don't*, my dress—"

"You have on my coat, Courtney, and we are going to be married in a little over a week. I'll lay out your clothes—there's no time to summon Mandy if you insist on going down. Now, get behind that screen—"

Ignoring her little sounds of protest, Clint struck a match on the heel of his boot. Courtney scampered behind the folding screen beside the closet just as the room was flooded with light.

Fortunately, the water pitcher and wash basin were nearby. Courtney could sponge her wounds. Later she would have Doc George disinfect them. Now her concern was being able to reach the closet door with a bare arm without its being detected. Well, Clint was gentleman enough to turn his gaze elsewhere. And he was preoccupied with questions as she pulled out the first garment within reach. Fortunately, it was the old-rose cashmere tea gown. The long sleeves, cuffed in ecru lace, would hide the scratches on her arms. There was no time to lace herself into a corset, but the inset belt would conceal the fact.

"Tell me *everything*!" Clint commanded.

In a voice often muffled by garments she struggled with, Courtney summarized quickly. "I—I was terrified—and nobody had told me about the strange house or the mill—"

"No," Clint said slowly, "and I should have explained, knowing that it was an old wound with Aunt Bella. That was once a part of the Villard holdings known as 'Rambling Gate.' When Gaston, Alexis' ex-father-in-law, fell heir to the property, he converted it into a so-called 'game room' so it took on the title of '*Gambling* Gate'—"

"And that's what bothered Cousin Bella?" Courtney asked as she struggled with the top button of her blouse's back opening.

"No—and I really shouldn't go into it, but Gaston Villard's sister was the woman Doc George married—do you know the story?"

There was no way to fit the stubborn buttonhole around the button. The dress would have to gape open!

"Yes, Cousin Bella has told me enough. But what," she wondered aloud, picking up the hairbrush, "was your brother doing there?"

"I really don't know—"

"What is *anybody* doing in that dreadful place? And who owns it now?"

Her hair was a tangled mess. Should she ask Clint to leave now? She needed the mirror. And dressing one's hair seemed such a private thing. While she hesitated behind the screen, Clint answered.

"I am not sure who owns Gambling Gate. Alexis tried to reclaim the land after the taxes were delinquent. It is possible that since she married his brother, Horace feels obligated to look in on the place."

Clint paused. Then, as if thinking aloud, he continued. "Of course, Milt's in jail and Alexis is not around—but you do know how greedy for property they are. I have heard that children sometimes play there if their parents don't know. The place is supposed to be inhabited by ghosts," he chuckled. And then he was serious again. "But children would not be there at night—the light's still a mystery."

Time was fleeting. Shyly, Courtney came from behind the screen to meet the admiring eyes of her husband-to-be.

"How beautiful, Courtney," he whispered huskily.

"With my hair like this? I—I guess I need to ask you to leave the room so I can comb the pinecones from it!"

"Here," Clint said authoritatively, "give me the brush. I can save us some time."

"I—Clint, I don't think it's proper."

In answer, he took the brush from her hand. "What's more, you are unbuttoned in back—"

"Clint, *no*—don't you *dare!*"

Clint laughed outright. "Want me to think you're going to be an untidy wife who cares nothing for her appearance once she has caught a man in her net? Stop squirming or I will be forced to use this brush elsewhere!"

Courtney sighed and sat down before the mirror. "I can see you are going to be the heavy-handed husband."

"No secret."

"And father?"

"Oh, yes, I will be cruel to our children. I will read to them unmercifully long, see that they memorize Bible verses, teach them to ride like the wind, and hug the life out of them—just like I will their mother."

Courtney, her heart bursting with happiness, watched his beloved reflection in the mirror as he tenderly ran the hairbrush through her long, raven mane. There was no pain, even as the hair snarled. Just as pain would be lessened as they attacked life's problems together. The fears of the day dissolved temporarily as the faint tinkle of a bell said, "Dinner!"

CHAPTER 10
Surprises

The next few days were filled with surprises. The first was a welcome letter from Lance, obviously written before Courtney's letter reached him. She found his letter troubling.

> Your mother behaves as though there were no other people around, isolating herself and calling them "tiresome." As a child, the Lady Ana was one of the golden goddesses who inhabited my world. Sadly, I watch the illusion fade. I do try, however, to bring a bit of joy into her life—being one of the few persons she will receive. She feels abandoned, although her exile is a condition of choice. She is lonely, restless, and strangely afraid of something intangible. Could it be living that frightens her?

Courtney let the letter drop into her lap. It was so sad. Mother, the beautiful woman who had possessed everything but love. If only she could have heard Brother Jim's sermon on Eternal Life, perhaps she would feel less depressed to see her youth slipping away. But, no, Courtney realized sadly, the message would have had little impact. The words Brother Jim used might well have applied to Mother's agnostic stance: "Jesus said, 'Ye have not the love of God in you.' "

It was good that Clint had offered to take her back to visit, Courtney thought. And then she wondered how long it would be before the weather allowed them to travel safely. Mother must resign herself to waiting, although patience was a virture she lacked. Poor, dear Mother. But she must not allow her mother's choices to interfere with the wedding. She would pray for Mother's depression to pass.

Feeling sad, as she always felt where Mother was involved, Courtney picked up Lance's letter and resumed:

It is amazing how quickly one can adjust, is it not, dear Courtney? I have resumed painting with a passion and have sold enough of my work that I am no longer among the "starving artists." Your portrait continues to dominate the scene—as you dominate my thoughts. I wish for you every known happiness, but I confess a certain regret that I allowed another man to take you from my childhood dreams . . . perhaps I should have fought harder. Just remember that I will always be your slave . . . only rub your magic ring . . . and I will come . . .

The tears that stained the rest of the letter were for her mother, for Lance, and for everybody else who had missed the kind of love she and Clint shared. "Bless them all, Lord," she whispered, "and bring somebody wonderful into each lonely life . . ."

*   *   *

Efraim was coming home Friday. All in all, his arrival was to be a special event. A time to complete plans for the wedding. And a time to reveal some secrets, Courtney and Mandy conspired—little knowing that Efraim would bring home some secrets of his own.

On Friday, the sun and clouds wrestled for right-of-way. At last, the sun surrendered and great snowflakes drifted lazily but persistently to earth. Occasionally, the vanquished sun, a silver tray in need of polishing, peered through the clouds momentarily to watch fencerows turn to marble as the peaks and gables of Mansion-in-the-Wild glistened like new silver. And then it retreated. The storm was too much. Courtney watched in fascination as a light wind slanted the snow like Mandy's wash billowing on the line. And she listened as the same wind murmured at the windows as if it, too, were whispering secrets. This meant a white Christmas. And Christmas meant that she would become Mrs. Clinton Desmond. Oh, such miracles as God wrought!

The murmurous drone of voices reminded her that there was work to do today. Dreaming must wait until next week when the exciting countdown began. For now, she must get into the kitchen . . .

Hours later, she looked out on a perfect night as she waited for Clint, Efraim, Brother Jim, and Doc George to arrive. One by one—in that order—they appeared and one by one Courtney ran out to greet them.

"Was there ever a night like this?" she whispered softly to Clint as, together, they looked at the sparkling heavens in their one moment alone.

The sky had cleared. An enormous-faced golden moon hung silent in the sequined veil of the Milky Way. But the stars paled in comparison to the shine of love that she read in Clint's face.

"The world is waiting for Christmas," he whispered, "Christmas and its message of love!"

The tinkle of Cousin Bella's dinner bell. And all moved forward as Donolar, his nose pink with cold, dumped an armload of wood by the hungry fireplace and then—glancing cautiously around—wiped his hands on the seat of his breeches. There was no indication that anybody saw.

And suddenly they were in the dining room. Tonight the table was draped with the handmade lace cloth Cousin Bella's grandmother had tatted for her hope chest. Courtney recognized it as one of the pieces clung to and stored away in the camphor chest. Just why her cousin chose to use it now, Courtney could never guess. But surely it signified something. How beautiful it was beneath the mellow glow of the candles. Between the candlesticks was Donolar's arrangement of balsam boughs and snowdrops from the forest. As Clint seated Courtney, Donolar rearranged a twig and murmured softly:

What is love? 'tis not hereafter;
Present mirth hath present laughter;
What's to come is still unsure . . .

Courtney smiled at him affectionately. Whatever her brother meant by the out-of-context quote from Shakespeare was as much a puzzle as himself. Time would reveal.

The next surprise was no surprise at all to Courtney and Mandy. But it overwhelmed the other diners and became a source of pride to Clint and blessings to them all.

Mandy and Mrs. Rueben had compromised on the bill of fare. The main dish would be the German housekeeper's *sauerbraten*, a great favorite of Mr. Clint's. But the bread was to be the cook's sourdough biscuits (*evahbody's* bes' loved) with sweet, morning-churned butter. Dessert?

"Mah biz'ness!" Mandy had declared and, with flashing eyes, shooed a sullen Mrs. Rueben from the kitchen.

Now the moment was at hand. Both stood at attention like tin soldiers as the others were seated. There was the customary silence as all eyes turned to Arabella Kennedy. With the dignity of a queen, she asked the usual question.

"Who wishes to read the Scripture this evening?"

"Ah duz!" Mandy's voice was humble but clear.

There was a moment of stunned silence before the hostess regained composure. "Go ahead, Mandy."

Mandy's faultlessly starched apron rustled as she reached behind her for an open Bible. Using a plump finger to trace the lines, she began: "De Lawd is mah shep'ahd . . ."

At first the mellow voice trembled and then it rose in triumph, reaching a volume that rivaled Brother Jim's by the time she finished reading the Twenty-third Psalm.

". . . 'n ah shall dwell in de house uv de Lawd forevah!"

The chorus of *Amens* was deafening. Cousin Bella wiped a tear from her eye. Donolar applauded with an abandon Courtney had never seen him use. The others were still in shock. Except for Clint, who reached for Courtney's hand.

And then, in true character, Brother Jim cleared his throat as if to dissolve an aggravating lump. "Now, Brothers and Sisters, let us praise the Lord in silence. To hear the Scriptures and not reflect upon them would be likened to eating Mandy's chocolate cake without tasting its sweetness!"

"I'll have you know *I* baked that cake!"

The minute the words were out, Courtney could have bitten off her tongue. She had spoiled Mandy's moment of glory. She had behaved unseemly. And she had broken into a sacred moment. Oh, what must they think of her?

But to her surprise there was a burst of laughter and then a round of applause. Then everybody was talking at once. *How did it happen? When? It was a miracle*, they said.

It was Donolar who observed, "Proof of the pudding lies in the tasting."

More laughter. Complete departure from the evening ritual. Courtney might as well add to it.

"Donolar's right. You may praise Mandy, but postpone opinion of dessert."

"If our sister baked it, it *has* to be good—right, Donolar?" Efraim said gallantly.

Courtney raised an eyebrow at Mandy who rolled her eyes toward the high, arched ceiling. Both were remembering that two of the layers were lopsided and that it had taken Mandy's know-how to conceal the fact by balancing highs and lows at the bottom of the seven-layer cake.

Doc George was hungry. "I'm with Donolar," he said above the din of voices. "Let's get to meditating so we can sample the wares."

"Amen!" said Brother Jim. "Praise the Almighty for the beauty of this pair—the ivory and the ebony of them! He knew from the beginning what He was doing, bringing them in harmony like the keys on a piano!"

All heads bowed.

When the evening drew to a close, Clint accompanied Courtney up the stairs. At the door of her bedroom he paused.

"You are a wonder, little Courtney," he whispered softly. "You will never know what you have brought to this house."

"You will never know what this house has brought to me!"

"Courtney, it's a whole week until the wedding—" Clint groaned, pulling her to him and resting his chin on her hair. "Let's elope!"

Courtney giggled and snuggled closer. "Did you like my cake that well?"

"Be serious! Can't you tell when a man's in love?"

Courtney's heart, like her feet, stood on tiptoe. But she forced her words to be light. "Elope! Cousin Bella would make stew of us—goodnight, my darling."

* * *

Courtney longed to stretch out luxuriously beneath the downy comforter and drop into the arms of sleep. With a tender smile that remembrance of the day brought, Courtney whispered a "Thank You, Lord" and closed her eyes.

But her day was not ended apparently. What was that? She sat up, wondering what had disturbed the serenity of the darkness. She tensed. Listened. But at first all she could hear were the fingers of the wind brushing the firs to emit low, somber notes like human hands upon a cello.

And then the sound again. This time identifiable. The almost inaudible whistle of a valley quail. Quails did not call in the night. Neither did they call at this season. It had to be Donolar.

Without lighting a lamp, Courtney thrust her feet into furry slippers and crept out the door and down the stairway.

Once outside, she called softly, "Donolar?"

There was no sound. But she could feel his presence. And the moon was her ally. Its slanting beams pointed out the cringing outline where he hid beneath the hedge. Obviously, he was scared out of his wits.

Courtney ran toward him, losing a slipper. "Oh darling, what is it?"

She could almost see the wide blue eyes, their lack of expression so out of place in the quivering, white face. And was the pounding her own heart or his? Probably both.

Avoiding the jagged rocks fencing the flower beds, she eased toward him and knelt. "We'll both freeze out here," she whispered between chattering teeth. "Come inside—"

"Oh, no!—*please*—I can't!" The desperate voice was so low Courtney could scarcely hear. "I—I've come to warn you—they're back—the evil ones—"

"The Bellevues? How do you know, Donolar?"

"I saw their lanterns—like evil eyes, they were swinging in the dark—back and forth—back and forth—"

"Are you sure of their identity? And did they try to harm you? We must alert the others—"

"Oh, no—*please*—I only wanted you to know—to keep my secret—because you are my sister and you understand."

"Efraim is your brother, darling. He loves you, too. He will understand—"

Donolar hesitated while Courtney held her breath. *Please, Lord*, her heart cried out silently.

And then her prayer was answered. Before Donolar reached a definite decision, Efraim noiselessly joined them. She had forgotten that his room across the hall gave him access to the sounds below while Clint's, so far removed, did not.

"What in the world—"

Donolar's frenzied "*Sh-h-h-h!*" caused him to pause and Courtney seized the advantage and summarized the situation.

"I see," Efraim said with obvious concern. "Any idea what they want, Donolar? Come inside with me and we'll talk—"

"Oh, no!" Donolar protested in a wild whisper. "I must go back to the Isle of Innisfree. The butterflies are sleeping—and if they should miss me and come looking, the evil ones would kill them—then I, too, should weep—"

At that point, he began babbling foolishly. And Efraim, thoroughbred that he was, put an arm about the thin shoulders of his brother and pulled him to his feet.

"I will walk home with you then and make sure that everything is safe. We will let nothing happen to you. That I promise!"

Donolar clung to Efraim as a child clings to a mother. "I believe you," Donolar said, "and so will the butterflies."

"They'd better!" Efraim said in a normal tone. "And now, little sister, get yourself back to bed! I refuse to give away a bride who sniffles and sneezes!"

Courtney was only too glad to do as she was told. So, forgetting her slipper, she ran back into the warmth and security of the Mansion. Wrapping a blanket around her, she sat waiting for Efraim. This might be their only opportunity to talk.

The waiting was longer than she expected. It was with relief that she saw his shadow emerge from the trees. And then the shadow became two! Courtney's heart quickened. What now? There was a quick exchange of words, the sound of muted footsteps, and then a knock on the door.

"Open, Sesame!"

Clint!

Without thinking, Courtney sprang from the chair. Stumbling over the blanket, then dropping it, she rushed to unlatch the door. She stopped just short of throwing herself into his arms, then—realizing that she was barefooted and clad only in her long flannel nightgown—she backed away.

"Wh—what—ever are you d-doing here? And we— I—n-not—dressed—" Courtney gasped between frozen lips.

"Sitting in the dark and freezing to death! Efraim, have you no control over this sister?"

"None! Get something on, Courtney!" Efraim ordered. "We're coming in."

Courtney ran gingerly over the cold floor and fumbled with the blanket, managing to drape it around her shivering body just as her brother lit a candle. Clint, she realized, was kneeling at her feet. What in the world was he doing in that silly position?

In spite of the questions that swarmed in her mind, Courtney found herself stifling a giggle at the melodrama. But she must make the situation no more foolish than it was. Had they all taken leave of their senses?

Candlelight flickered on Clint's hair revealing the masculine beauty of his face. She longed to reach out and brush the rebellious kink of sun-burnished hair from his forehead. The thought of touching him turned amusement to love.

"What *are* you doing here, Clint?" she asked softly. "It must be past midnight!"

"Well past. So you see, I was unable to sleep after tonight's ball. A beautiful face kept haunting me and I was unable to seek sweet repose until I found the lovely princess who had lost her slipper."

Her house slipper! Their voices must have disturbed him. He came down to investigate and—

"Hold out your foot!"

"I will not—*Efraim!*"

"Who am I to interfere with a wedding?" her brother said in amusement. "It is my duty to marry you off!"

And suddenly Clint's hand spanned her slender ankle, his thumb and forefinger almost meeting, and slipped the fuzzy shoe onto her foot.

"You're bold!" Courtney said, wriggling her cold toes gratefully against the fleece lining. "Very bold."

"Not bold—masterful! And you'll grow to love it!"

I love it already, her heart cried out. But Efraim reminded them of his presence with a discreet cough. " 'If the shoe fits, wear it,' but not to your wedding! Now, with that settled, can we get down to business?"

The three of them talked until sleepy night birds warned of approaching day. How wonderful it was, Courtney thought, for Efraim to be a part of this warm, informal family. They talked about the wedding and about Donolar's fears. When Clint claimed to be as hungry as "an owl in the wilderness" and went cautiously to the kitchen for milk and some of Mandy's molasses cookies, Courtney told Efraim of their mother's request that she come back "home." For how long? Courtney was uncertain—maybe to stay. She was very wise, Efraim said, to tell Mother of their wedding plans. She was about to tell him of Clint's offer to accompany her for a visit when Clint arrived from his raid of the kitchen.

"Have you told Efraim about your sightings at Gambling Gate?" Clint asked, handing her a glass of milk. "Drink this. Doc George says you're no more than skin, bones, and a hank of hair. 'What kind of mother will she make?' he asks."

"I'm fit as a fiddle, as Cousin Bella says when he asks her to hold out her tongue. And I have a good appetite!"

To prove it, Courtney drained the glass and reached for a cookie. She told Efraim then of her frightening experience, carefully omitting the appearance of Horace Bellevue.

"Then Donolar's imagination may not have run rampant. Maybe he saw something after all—something significant. It so happens that I will be checking things out—" Efraim's voice was thoughtful and he seemed about to elaborate then changed the subject abruptly. "I have some news of my own—something I intended sharing at dinner. But the meal brought surprises of its own—"

"Tell us, Efraim. This is a better time," Clint urged.

Courtney swallowed and almost choked in her haste to swallow the rest of her cookie. "Yes—tell us!" she gulped.

Both men had seated themselves on opposite sides of Courtney. Now Efraim rose from his chair and paced the floor restlessly.

"So many things have happened," he said at length, running nervous fingers through the thickness of his near-gold hair. "Details are unimportant, I guess, but remember how indecisive I was when the two attorneys-at-law returned to the East and wanted me to go along?"

Courtney remembered only too well. And now her heart stood still.

"I just might have gone except for your impending wedding—and now, something has come up that makes it appear that I will be staying—"

"Oh, Efraim!" Courtney leaped from her chair, forgetting the blanket, and reached up to embrace him.

Clint, too, had risen and was extending his hand which Efraim accepted from within the circle of Courtney's arms. Then the three of them laughed and returned to their chairs while Efraim continued with his news.

"A very learned man, a semi-retired attorney who has a number of interesting cases to his credit, has come to the city and would like a younger man to go into business with him. I never thought such a break would come my way. Imagine working with the proverbial 'Philadelphia lawyer'!"

"The good break works both ways, I'd say," Clint said heartily. "Who is the man and what brought him here?"

"His name is VanKoten, Robert VanKoten, American-born, educated in Europe, excellent background. He has had holdings here for some time—looked after by his daughter—"

"A daughter? Efraim, are you telling us everything?"

At her question, Courtney thought her brother's color deepened in the candlelight. But Efraim's voice was steady when he answered. "I have only met Miss Van-Koten once and she appears to be a nice young lady. Now

Courtney, control that flight of fantasy. This is business, strictly business."

Young. Nice. Unmarried. Courtney wished she knew more about Miss VanKoten. But the men were talking and she listened.

"Aunt Bella will be pleased," Clint was saying.

"She knows," Efraim replied. "You see, Mr. VanKoten and I are working on some of her legal affairs—we're in business already in a rather inadequate office while the other one is under construction. Money seems to be no object on my senior partner's part. He insists on setting up the business on his own even though I offered to negotiate a loan. He never had a son so welcomes the chance to help me get a real start. Right now we are working on a personal matter for him—trying to locate the rightful owners to Gambling Gate."

"Gambling Gate!" Clint was obviously surprised.

"The same. Mr. VanKoten would like to restore it and return the old landmark to its original name as well, Rambling Gate. I foresee many a challenge."

* * *

On Saturday Courtney helped Mandy with the Sunday baking. Doc George stopped by on his way to check a leg he had splinted for the Laughtens' horse. As usual, he visited the spice-scented kitchen and, as usual, was welcomed. Cutting two thick slices of Mandy's black-crust bread, he generously spread them with butter.

"Arabella's not up to par. Worry, worry," he grumbled. "So today's medicine's a little humoring. Will you pour me two cups of coffee? Then I'll listen to her latest problem. We all need more ears and a shorter tongue!"

Mandy refused to let Courtney dirty her "purty hands afore de weddin' 'n all." So Courtney took her leave and started upstairs to write about the strange happenings of late in her journal. There was no way to bypass the sun room. And even in passing hurriedly by she saw and overheard enough to alert her that something else was in the making. Not so much what she heard as what she did not hear. And not what she saw, but what she imagined.

"—much rather you gave it up, Arabella. We've buried the past. Don't exhume it. If you'd listen to reason the two of us could be getting on with the future—"

Arabella Kennedy's voice was stronger than the doctor had described her condition. "It's important to me, George Washington—important to the children—the property being dangerously near—"

Courtney tried to hurry past. But without a turn of her head she saw Doc George lean forward and brush Cousin Bella's pink cheek with a kiss . . .

CHAPTER 11
The Sunday of Surrender

Efraim attended church with the family on Sunday. Since the wedding was exactly one week from today, he needed to get his bearings—know precisely how many paces there were from the door to the pulpit so he could escort his sister down the aisle properly, he said.

Courtney was delighted. She hoped with all her heart that Brother Jim would deliver one of his better sermons.

The sun disappeared behind a thin layer of clouds as the buggies rolled along. But Courtney's high spirits were undaunted. Seated between Clint and Efraim, one arm linked affectionately in Efraim's on her right and Clint's on her left, she concentrated on the beauty of the morning—the first day of her wedding week! As if picking up her mood, the clouds gathered color from the sun they sought to obscure, their luminous pink trailing reflected brilliance over the surface of the river as it outran the turning wheels. There was no wind, but the snowcapped mountains were all but obscured in a misty tulle. Their gentle warning of approaching rain.

There was only one bad moment to spoil the day. It happened at an inopportune time when a crowd had congregated around Courtney, teasing for tidbits as a preview to the forthcoming wedding. Courtney kept shaking her head and saying it was all a secret—and had they met her "other brother"? The women had not. Many of the men had. The loggers. The miners. The trappers, farmers, and businessmen. Most, Efraim explained later, had been to him for legal advice regarding the filing of claims, homesteading laws, or seeking help on having an occasional hint of gold here and there assayed. It was obvious that Efraim was well-received.

It should have been a joyous moment. And it was until Courtney's eyes spotted the unmistakable figure of Alexis Worthington Villard Bellevue emerging from the church. She flaunted indifference toward the settlers much as she flaunted her body movements, moving with studied rhythm and allowing a filmy scarlet scarf to trail behind her. Indifferent or not, her jeweled fingers reached up to sweep dark locks from her equally dark eyes. In them, Courtney read a searching look. Unreasoning anger clasped Courtney's throat. The shame of this woman! What was she doing here? And who was the object of her search? She had made her stage entrance and the woman jolly well better leave it there. One look at Clint—

But it was Efraim on whom Alexis centered her gaze. She waved boldly, smiled invitingly, and disappeared. Efraim tipped his hat politely. But he looked a little perplexed as he turned to resume his conversation with the men.

Questions flooded Courtney's mind. But they were soon forgotten in the sanctity of the church where she had come to know Christ as her personal Savior. It seemed preordained, she thought with a rush of love, that she should surrender her life to Clint here. Oh, that everybody in the world could know such happiness!

And then, seated between Clint and Efraim, Courtney lost herself in the worship service. "My text for the day comes from Isaiah 12:5: 'Sing unto the Lord, for he hath done excellent things'—so sing out good brothers and sisters, sing out the glory of His name. If you don't know the words, you ladies hum and you men whistle!"

What followed was a beautiful symphony of music,

sweeter by far than that which Courtney remembered as Chamber Music which her mother often arranged for parties at Waverly Manor. Remembering the words from previous meetings, Courtney sang the words with Clint. And it warmed her heart to hear Efraim whistle as the melody filled the church:

> Down at the cross where my Savior died,
> Down where for cleansing from sin I cried,
> There to my heart was the blood applied;
> Glory to His name!
> Glory to His name . . . Glory to His name . . .

Brother Jim readied himself for his battle with sin, loosening his tie and doubling his fists as if to knock out his opponent in the first punch. "Is it well with thee?"

The chorus of *Amens* responding to the bellowed question shook the rafters. "Making sure it is! The Lord's in need of no crossover Christians—worshiping their Maker on Sunday and following the Deluder for the next six days! No need for neutrality either. He'll spew you right out of His mouth—the Good Book says so—if you're neither hot nor cold. And the hypocrite? Alas, Babylon! Woe be unto him who claims to be a Christian soldier because he sits tall in the saddle—never mind the destination. God needs reckless Christians. You may not understand Him and His ways. You may not be able to explain Him. But you answer His call and you can follow as recklessly as that first wagon train of settlers. He's sick of the Doctor Feelgoods—"

He paused, took a dipper of water from the bucket at his side, and sized up the congregation. As was his pattern, Brother Jim softened his tone then. "It takes courage. It takes downright *guts*! But how can you lose with God on your side? Love is always reckless, daring—

even dangerous—but oh, dear brothers and sisters, if you want a glimpse of the reward, have a look at the faces of Clint Desmond and Courtney Glamora! They're reckless in their love, plunging into the new life together, their hearts singing 'Glory to His Name'!"

There was wild applause. Courtney felt tears gather and spill over as Clint reached for her hand. She dared not look at Efraim. She was unable even to formulate a proper prayer. But the Lord understood. And so did Efraim. With a squeeze of her hand, he was on his way to the altar.

Courtney, Clint, and Efraim left ahead of the rest of the family. Cousin Bella remained to discuss plans for a quilting bee, the wedding, and the reception following at Mansion-in-the-Wild.

"Oh, Efraim, I'm so proud of you!" Courtney burst out, her spirits undampened by the warning drops of rain.

Efraim looked thoughtful. "Don't be—not just yet. I'm just a novice. It will take me a long time to catch up—and, although I know that I made the right decision, I—well, hang it all! I question my own faith. Maybe I don't have enough—"

Courtney's heart went out to him. She remembered the same doubts. But how could she make him understand?

It was Clint who put it into words. Words which surely must have come straight from above. "You have no need of a greater faith, Efraim. It is not your great faith that will see you through. It is faith in the great God in our everyday lives."

How beautiful. Courtney felt a rush of tenderness and love bathe her, turning the rain to liquid sunshine.

The men went on talking, but she did not hear. Not at first. And then Clint's offhand comment caught her attention.

"I was unaware that you knew Alexis Bellevue."

Efraim seemed to hesitate before answering, "I don't —at least not very well. I failed to recognize her at first. Mrs. Bellevue came to me for professional advice— something that worries me a little. But I will surrender that to the Lord!"

CHAPTER 12
Mixed Emotions

This should be the happiest week of her life. And in many ways—the ways that counted, Courtney supposed—it was. Certainly, her forthcoming marriage sent thrills of pure joy coursing through her veins. She was counting the hours until she and Clint were one and in the few spare moments allowed her in the feverish pitch of preparations, she—like some lovesick schoolgirl—practiced writing: "Courtney Glamora Desmond," "Mrs. Clinton Desmond," and "Clint and Courtney."

Her heart filled with joy, too, at Efraim's profession of faith. His faith would grow just as his love for Clint's "Dream Country" had grown. As Clint had said so often, "Every day we look at this glorious land, we feel the mighty hand of God leading us on to greater things." It was happening in her own life already in a million ways. And now, one by one, that Mighty Hand was reaching out to those she loved and drawing them into His own Great Circle.

How she longed to share these thoughts with Mother. Her heart was heavy with longing for the mother she had never really understood. Was it possible that deep down inside her mother burned a spark of love for Courtney? Could the letter urging Courtney's return mean a softening?

No, she must not entertain such a hope. She must accept Mother as she was. Self-centered. Vain. And willing to stoop to any means to an end that would satisfy her own selfish purpose. Poor Mother. She would be unable to understand this land or its people, or Courtney's love for Clint, whom her mother would see as a "beggarly miner." And least of all would she be able to understand their newfound faith. So there was no need to put the beautiful thoughts on paper. They would only serve to further Mother's distress. Mother, Courtney thought guiltily, had undoubtedly fallen into a swoon upon receiving her last letter.

Mother's condition preyed upon Courtney's mind and she was comforted only by the fact that Mother was not being neglected. Lance was looking in on her frequently. Efraim was sending her money. And it was not as if she had refused Mother's plea. She would be paying her a visit when she was Mrs. Clinton Desmond!

That set the blood crowding back into her heart with such force that she felt light-headed. Before her eyes swam the vision of Clint taking his vows—his eyes sparkling as blue water sparkles in the sunlight.

No, she could never write these thoughts to Mother. But she could post them in her journal. She could write, "My heart sings to You, Lord, for the sun and all its glory—and You will forgive me if I say that for me it rises and sets in Clint's shoes?" God would understand.

But there were other matters that troubled Courtney. Questions left unanswered. Some of them which she hesitated to voice. Others which sent thrills of horror down her spine. There, admittedly, were times when her imagination ran rampant . . . when she felt desperate . . . driven in some unexplainable way, never knowing what direction or by whom . . . and somewhat desperate in her anxiety.

Smaller matters concerned Efraim's partner. Wasn't the name Robert VanKoten? It seemed strange that such a learned man would come to Washington Country and seek out a partner. Courtney wondered what business he was having Efraim investigate and, for that matter, exactly what Efraim was taking care of for Cousin Bella. Did it concern her will? There was certainly no rush. And what was it that Doc George had asked Cousin Bella to forego? But, most of all, where her brother was concerned, Courtney wondered what Alexis wanted of him. Was there any connection? Probably not.

And certainly not to her apprehensions either. Nothing was going to stop the wedding. Nothing! And, yet, as she tried to reassure herself, Courtney felt a sense of panic . . . as if she were groping in some haunted house, not knowing what horror lay ahead. And then she recognized the house . . . Gambling Gate!

CHAPTER 13
Beloved Stranger

Christmas Eve!

Courtney awoke early. Even so, the softly muted voices and the mellow aroma of freshly brewed coffee tattled that Mandy and Mrs. Rueben were up. Maybe, she thought with a smile as she looked between the folds of the heavy drapes at the patch of starry sky, the peace of Christmas would steal into their hearts, allowing the two to make it through this day without conflict.

Hope, like an iridescent bubble (and just as short-lived, she was to find) enlarged in her heart. In her ecstatic state of mind, Courtney decided that some of the fears that had gripped her were born of her fertile imagination. She and Donolar were cut from the same cloth. Could it be that their sensitive natures led them astray? Made small incidents into one of Grandma McCreary's Medicine Show "mellerdrammers"? Well—it was possible. *Anything* was at this time. So if she could imagine evil, she could imagine good! Nothing could jeopardize this day. And, she thought with a pounding heart, this *night!* Clint had reserved a room at Ma Becker's *Chateau* (the city's most elegant, since it boasted inside plumbing). There they were to spend three golden days—72 hours—together. *Alone!*

"Stop it!" Courtney giggled to herself. "A little more of such dreaming and you'll be too weak-kneed to walk down the aisle!"

There were last-minute details to which she must attend. But the invitation of the coffee was too much.

Sticking a tentative foot from beneath the covers, she searched the cold darkness of the floor for her slippers. Her teeth were chattering as she dug her toes into their furry lining. Then gratefully she wrapped herself in a floor-length flannel bathrobe. With as little noise as possible, in case Cousin Bella was still sleeping, she crept down the stairs. Mandy greeted her with open arms.

"Miz Courtney! Honey, y'all hadn't oughta be up dis early, it bein' de day heben's bells is a-gonna ring fo' y'n Mistah Clint. Mistah Clint he dun went to' be wid Mistah Efraim till de weddin', cuz he ain't 'lowed t'see de bride. Heah, set yo'sef down 'n get some uv Mandy's hot coffee t'warm yo' insides—'n sit close by de oben uv de cookstove. A no'ther dun blowed in las' night—a real Chris'mus feel. Mistah Clint laid de fiahs throughout de house, but dey ain't yet lighted—drink whilst I buttah y'all uh biscit!"

Courtney warmed her hands on the mug, then took a hot, bracing swallow. But she was too excited to eat. So Clint was with Efraim . . . and would meet her at the altar . . .

*   *   *

It was a beautiful wedding, one the valley folk would talk about to their grandchildren. "You shudda seen the church—not a wall in sight, all decked out in evergreens 'n wild-rose hips," they would say. "That kinda odd brother of th' bride was a genius in some ways—arrangin' th' candles 'mid mistletoe 'n no flowers a'tall. Why? Likely so Miz Courtney—Miz Desmond, the bossman's lady's—bouquet of Christmas roses'd show. Like I said, a kind of genius that boy was—not a housewife hereabouts could've produced such flowers at that time a'year!"

Of course, there were a few questions, they admitted. Like who was that fifty-aged gentleman with the goatee beard and dressed fit t' be killed? There was a prettyish-like young lady beside him. Strange they never showed up at th' big shindig afterwards—just up and disappeared like that woman wearin' a dress redder'n a ball o'yarn. Her face was familiar. Oh, th' shindig afterwards? Just you wait! That was the strangest night ever . . .

Courtney was aware of none of the whisperings. She had walked in a dream since Cousin Bella had slipped the filmy silk mull wedding dress over her dark head, murmuring over and over, "You're a beautiful bride, my child—beautiful—and how I envy you!" Then, with a sigh, "I had hoped to have a suitable wedding gift—a very special legacy which perhaps will come later. But I did arrange to have the organ taken to the church. If conditions were less unsettled, I would leave it there. As it is—oh, Courtney, how beautiful you are—and what your mother is missing! There, go see for yourself."

Courtney remembered looking at herself in the long mirror above the low marble-topped table in Cousin Bella's bedroom. And there she saw a reflection that she failed to recognize. The beautiful vision in the billowing skirt with filmy lace cupping her face could not be herself. Mother had always thought her plain. How then the transformation? Cara's perseverance, her ripping and starting over time and time again, that's what did it. And now the dress transformed her. She saw reflected the face of a beautiful stranger. A stranger over whose head was being placed a dainty cap threaded with seed pearls from which flowed a frothy veil. The cap that had belonged to another bride-to-be so long ago. Could it be Cousin Bella she was seeing and not Courtney Glamora?

If so, the wedding would never occur . . .

The ride to the Church-in-the-Wildwood was wiped from her memory like the markings on a slate. And only vaguely did she recall taking Efraim's arm and walking slowly . . . slowly . . . slowly toward Brother Jim. That was when the tall bronzed stranger appeared. His face was familiar—perhaps because of the rebellious lock of hair that kept falling over the beautiful face. So strong. So practical. So down-to-earth. While she was the dreamer . . . the hopeless romantic.

And then she saw the love shining in his eyes, those blue, blue eyes focused on her, his chosen bride. Oh, the miracle of this day! Oh, the miracle of Christmas! Out of all the women in the world, this man had chosen her! This beloved stranger whom God was making hers.

The fragrance of evergreens . . . the soft strains of organ music . . . a few whispers . . . and, in comical contrast, the snort of somebody blowing his nose.

"Do you, Clinton, take this woman to be your lawful wedded wife?"

"I do."

The words rang out like a shot in the hush of the church. Clint! Oh the eagerness of his voice . . .

"And do you, Courtney—"

Courtney stood paralyzed for a moment. Then there was a warm squeeze of her hand. Supporting. Encouraging. The hand of her husband-to-be. The hand that would forever hold her heart.

"I do, oh, *I do!*" she cried triumphantly.

And then, violating all rules laid down so carefully by Arabella Kennedy at the rehearsal, Mrs. Clinton Desmond threw her arms around her husband and kissed him hard before Brother Jim pronounced them husband and wife!

CHAPTER 14
The Night of the Wedding

❧

Gone was the bravado with which Courtney had taken her vows. She now felt constrained as oceans of people surged forth like a tidal wave. Some kissing the bride. Others pumping Clint's hand. And all of them banging on pots and pans in what they called a "shivaree."

Courtney's eyes met Clint's imploringly. "What on earth?"

Her question was drowned out by the noise, but Clint understood. "A mock serenade for newlyweds—we're supposed to smile—"

Then his voice, too, was lost in the tumult.

The noise bothered Courtney for some reason she would have found impossible to explain. A crashing crescendo announcing the rise of the curtain to a Shakespearean tragedy. She tried to console herself by remembering that such rising volume came before a comedy, too.

Nevertheless, she was relieved when at last she was seated beside Clint and ready for departure. No matter that theirs was the lead buggy by unanimous acclamation so there would be no "spoonin'—leastwise not yet!"

As the buggy moved forward, Courtney was only dimly aware that a never-ending caravan followed. That teasing eyes focused on their every move. And boisterous singing filled the forest. She was with Clint—her *husband*!

Her luminous eyes met Clint's. And, taking the reins in one hand, he managed to pull the lap robe up as a shield.

Then, almost reverently, he picked up her left hand, circled with a gentle forefinger the gold wedding band so recently slipped on below the pearl engagement ring, kissed the moist palm. And, ignoring the hoots and jeers behind them, with a ragged breath, he drew her close and kissed her tenderly.

Courtney's heart caught in her throat. She felt suspended, afloat with the spell of wonder. So this was what it was like to have a "lawful wedded husband"!

And then, all too soon, the Mansion-in-the-Wild loomed up to remind them that there was a day crowded with people ahead. A day so carefully and lovingly planned by family and friends. A day when, for the first time, Mr. and Mrs. Clinton Desmond would "receive." Then tonight was theirs . . .

"I'll help you change, Miz—I mean, Courtney," Cara offered and followed Courtney up the stairs.

Courtney, who had said good-bye reluctantly to Clint, made small talk with Cara, as she allowed herself to be buttoned into a pale blue serge suit, piped in old-rose to match the high-necked lace blouse.

"Ready-made, ain't it?" Cara Laughten breathed in admiration. When Courtney nodded, Cara said in address to herself, "I ain't never had me anything ready-made—"

Courtney's eyes filled with tears. It had been an emotional day and Cara's words touched her deeply. "No store could boast as beautiful a wedding gown as you made for me, Cara—I just wish there were some way I could repay you."

But Cara did not hear. She had caught sight of the long navy-blue gloves and matching pillbox hat Mandy had laid out for Courtney's "goin' away." Cara's fingers were caressing the blue dotted veil.

"Hemstitched—oh, I never, ever saw nothin' equalin' it—"

"The veil? Oh, Cara, I have another almost like it. It will be my pleasure to give it to you!"

Courtney rummaged quickly through the drawer of the Chippendale chifforobe and handed an astonished Cara a circle of filmy chiffon.

Their eyes met. Neither spoke. But their warm embrace spoke a language women in love understand.

Downstairs the noise had resumed. It was time for the newlyweds to greet their friends.

Courtney, a vision in blue and still carrying her bouquet of Christmas roses, walked slowly down the stairs. There was a hush as she paused at the landing. It was expected, Cousin Bella had coached her, that the bride toss her bouquet before the reception. That way it could serve as a centerpiece for the dining table before it was carried home by the girl lucky enough to catch it—indisputably the next bride of the settlement.

Thousands of faces—or was it millions?—looked up in open admiration and equal expectation. This was a great moment. A time to admire the bride. And a time for the parents of eligible daughters to fantasize. Not that they put much strength in the custom, mind you—but then, who knew?

Savoring the moment, Courtney let her eyes drink in the beauty of the scene. Donolar had outdone himself. Festoons of evergreen, mingled with bright sprigs of bittersweet, swung from the high-beamed ceiling. Holly and mistletoe entwined the banisters of the stairway. An enormous fir tree, its top branches brushing the ceiling, waited patiently in the corner until it was time to adorn it. And then her eyes met Clint's and locked. With no sense of direction, she flung the bridal bouquet and almost ran down the next flight and into his waiting arms.

Nestling there, Courtney wondered what could have caused all the commotion. The laughter and applause was thunderous! Then, wonder of wonders, Dr. George Washington Lovelace, with an affectionate arm around Cousin Bella's shoulders, was shaking with laughter.

"Ladi—ees, and gentlemen!" he barked with the aplomb of a street hawker, "meet the next bride-to-be!"

"Stuff and nonsense!" Cousin Bella's voice was less in control than she would have liked, it was easy to see. And that added to the merriment.

"Arrange this on the table, Donolar—and let's serve the meal!"

Arabella Kennedy was herself again, the mistress of the Mansion. And the crowd was hungry. Clint and Courtney smiled knowingly. Their shared relative had deftly turned the focus of attention from herself.

Again the dream descended. Courtney was aware of the enormity of the white wedding cake . . . the tables moaning and groaning with wild turkey, browned to perfection, pumpkin pie buried beneath mountains of whipped cream and a collection of vegetable dishes ranging from hearty German casseroles to French delicacies, to Mandy's mustard greens . . . and people, of equal variety, waiting to gobble up food as the roaring fires gobbled wood to set the rooms aglow . . . Brother Jim's beautiful prayer praising God for the miracle of Christmas and then comparing the love of husband and wife to that of Christ for His Church . . . and all the while Clint's loving gaze . . .

And then came the magical moment. It was time to light the candles on the Christmas tree! Mrs. Rueben, on signal, drew the heavy drapes. It was that move, shutting away the outside world, that blinded the merrymakers to the forthcoming danger.

CHAPTER 15
"In a Tumultuous Privacy of Storm"

Children gleefully strung the lower branches of the tree with strands of popcorn and Christmas-colored paper chains while their fathers draped the upper boughs and hung a shining star on the topmost peak. All the while, there was a fantasia of unrestricted voices joined in "O, Come All Ye Faithful."

Another prayer. And then the room was flooded with the light of a million candles, rivaling the brilliancy of the stars—had there been any lighting the sky.

If there had been a hint of storm, the wedding party had failed to notice as they rode merrily from the church to the Mansion beneath a windswept sky. Oh, true, the smithy had muttered that the wind had shifted. That a real "nor'easter could brang down th' snow." But wasn't Ahab's weather sense prone to be as dark as the smut on his leather apron? Why should a body be concerned over one threatening cloud?

But now that one cloud had become a grave reality—unbeknownst to the wedding party. At first, behind the damask drapes, only the windows were starred by snow. Then came a premature darkness with tree trunks casting gray-blue shadows on the thin carpet of white. The wind rose, but its hoarse voice was drowned out by the singers. Then, as if tired of its warning, the wind retreated into the forest, bending treetops earthward, and driving needles of snow against their trunks, shaping into drifts, and blotting out traces of any trail or bush that served as a landmark.

It was Donolar, with his special sixth sense, who opened a drape, letting in a crack of white light. Without change of expression, he began chanting softly:

> Announced by all the trumpets of the sky,
> Arrives the snow; and, driving o'er the fields,
> Seems nowhere to alight; the whited air
> Hides hills and woods, the river, and the
>   heaven,
> And veils the farm-house at the garden's end.

Looking slightly perplexed that nobody listened, Donolar raised his voice. The uncharacteristic gesture caught Courtney's ear. Something was wrong, she knew, and she hurried to her brother's side.

"What is wrong, darling? Tell me."

"I like Emerson," he said vaguely, still holding the drape:

> The sled and traveler stopped, the courier's
>   feet
> Delayed, all friends shut out, the housemates
>   sit
> Around the fireplace, enclosed
> *In a tumultuous privacy of storm.*

And then Courtney knew. Her cry of dismay halted the festivities. All crowded to the windows. The rest was bedlam.

* * *

What seemed like hours later, although it was a matter of minutes, Clint had the situation under control. At least, he had the men organized.

With the same quiet authority he used at the mines, Clint restored order. "Men," he said, "there is a need for organizing—for recognizing that there is no real threat to our families unless we panic. First, let's have a look outside—estimating the storm as best we can and planning from there—see if we can outrun the dark!"

White-faced, the women waited. They were accustomed, Courtney knew, to surrendering their husbands to duty here on the frontier. She was not. And certainly not on her wedding night! Resentment crept into her heart uninvited. Immediately it was banished. To be the wife she had promised God she would be meant rising to the occasion—*now*!

Forcing a smile to her lips, she said, "Clint will find a way—he'll take no unnecessary chances. Hasn't he proven that at the mines?"

Yes, the best bossman ever. And visibly they relaxed.

The door burst open letting in a blast of frigid air. The report was grim. Families whose homesteads were on this side of the creek could make it—with help. Clint and Efraim, being familiar with the trail used as a shortcut to the mines, would go ahead . . . guide them.

And You guide ME, Lord . . . I'm not sure I'm up to this, Courtney whispered in her heart.

The families on the other side of the creek? Well—it was impossible to find the bridge in this storm. Besides, it might collapse beneath such a burden of snow. Too risky.

"Then we're stranded?" One woman's voice rose hysterically.

Cousin Bella's back stiffened. "Nobody is stranded," she declared. "You're simply invited to spend Christmas at the Mansion-in-the-Wild!"

There was immediate calm. Arabella Kennedy had spoken. And her words brought an unexpected blessing from the storm. Imagine spending a night *here* . . .

Courtney wondered if Cousin Bella's courage would waver when Doc George announced that he would go along. He knew the trail, too. Oughtn't he now—considering how many summoned him from his warm bed in the wee hours to deliver their offspring? Unlikely, but there could be a need for his services.

Cousin Bella showed no emotion. But she worked her way through those bundling themselves for the journey ahead to stand by his side. "God go with you, George Washington," Courtney heard her say. Then, turning back to Courtney, "Now—you and I have some planning to do. This will give you a foretaste of what it's like to be the mistress of the Mansion.

Brother Jim would remain with the group here—sort of "shepherding the flock." But the look he cast Courtney's way caused her blood to run cold. She knew immediately that he was aware of the strange happenings at Gambling Gate. If he sensed danger, she should tell Clint—

Only Clint was dressed in heavy clothing, his face all but obscured by the woolen scarf below the stocking cap, and wearing practical snow boots. He was leaving!

"An' John's gonna go with 'im," Cara Laughten took her hand in effort to give strength—or gain it.

"But you live on *this* side, Cara—"

Cara nodded. "But," she said with white-faced pride, "my John's always there when they's a need."

"And we'll be here, too, Cara—waiting."

And then Clint was holding her breathlessly close. "Yes, wait, my darling—this night's not finished—"

Lanterns lighted, the leadmen stepped out. They walked ahead, their faces braced against the wind. The wagons followed. And the storm closed in around them . . .

* * *

Trying to calm herself, Courtney fled from the room, murmuring something about changing her clothes. In the privacy of her bedroom, she longed to throw herself across the bed and cry until her heart was wrung dry. But there was work to do. She had promised Clint she would be waiting. But not with idle hands! Squeezing back the tears, she stripped off the long, navy-blue gloves, removed her hat and put it carefully away in the hatbox, and ran a brush through her heavy tresses. Chin held high, she descended the stairs, unaware of how very like Arabella Kennedy she looked.

"What can I do?" Courtney asked unceremoniously.

"You, my dear, are now in a position to *give* orders."

"Oh, no!" Courtney said spiritedly, keeping her voice low. "You have a right to plan our future but not our present. Now, with that settled—"

Cousin Bella's laugh rang out, causing the others to look at her inquiringly. "Spoken like a true Glamora!" she whispered to Courtney, then to the others, "I was just thinking that we can make this house ring with laughter—could be our best Christmas ever!"

"Amen!" said Brother Jim. "Now, men, let's jump in the ring and figure our strategy. This is Christmas, like Sister Kennedy's said. And Christmas began with a Child—so what're we going to do for these children, making it well with them? Don't they deserve gifts?"

Why, Courtney thought, *we have given the children no thought at all.*

"Bobsleds!" Donolar cried out excitedly. "The boys should have bobsleds for riding in the snow. I have boards and nails and saws—"

Immediately he was surrounded by small boys, causing his face to shine like a rising star. The men had no choice but to follow at Donolar's heels. His moment of glory had come.

In the commotion that followed, Courtney found little time to think of her disappointment. There was more wood to be brought in. (Make a note of that, Courtney, when the men return.) Fresh coffee to make. (Clint, Efraim, Doc George, and John would be frozen.) And food? Yes, Mandy and Mrs. Rueben must warm the left-overs for a midnight feast. Cousin Bella and Courtney organized the women as Clint had organized the men.

"I will open the east tower, although goodness knows it will be dusty. We may need the room for sleeping quarters," Cousin Bella thought aloud. "Courtney, see that Mandy and Mrs. Rueben are behaving themselves in the kitchen, then we will need their help dragging out quilts and comforters. We've a lot of overnight guests!"

Courtney made no answer as there was a small tug at her skirt. Looking down, she saw the face of what looked like a miniature Christmas angel—a fairy-like creature with cornsilk-smooth golden hair and enormous eyes.

Courtney stooped to hear the wee voice say, "Don' us girls git nothin'?"

Courtney scooped the little creature into her arms, wondering to which lucky mother she belonged. "Of course you do, darling," she whispered, praying that she could somehow make the rash promise in her voice a reality.

Cara saved the night. Apparently having overheard, she said, "Ask her if a rag doll'll do. I had my John brang th' machine case'n something went wrong with th' wed-din' dress—"

"I praise the Lord for you, Cara!" Courtney murmured, brushing the other woman's cheek with a kiss.

Cara blushed modestly (and looked as honored as if the Queen of England had curtsied to her, Cousin Bella said later).

Minutes later, bright scraps of material appeared from nowhere. Cara's sewing machine whirred merrily. And other mothers were busily snipping, basting, and embroidering in a frenzy of excitement. Mandy popped corn and set the children to stringing it while she made popcorn balls.

"Keep de li'l angels outa y'all's haih," she confided with a wide grin of conspiracy, while to the children she said, "Y'all bein' good, you's gonna git play purties—bein' bad all y'all be gittin' iz switches in yore stockin's."

The children giggled as they huddled around the giant cookstove. Blissfully unaware of the wind which moaned like a grieving ghost, they whispered among themselves about the good fortune that allowed them to stay up past bedtime, " 'specially on Chris'mas Eve!"

But Courtney was aware. Above the hum of voices, she listened as the grandfather clock chimed six. Cousin Bella's dinner hour. Arabella Kennedy ignored the signal. Courtney, every nerve strained to hear the sound of a step on the front porch, waited tensely for the cuckoo clock, always late, to echo the report.

Seven . . . eight . . . *nine*. At ten o'clock Cousin Bella announced that it was time for coffee and prayer.

"Aren't we almost finished? And I expect to see the men come touting bobsleds any minute now—it's for—for the others we must pray."

Thimbles and spools rolled to the floor. Needles found their way to pincushions. And the women knelt by their chairs. It was thus that Brother Jim, Donolar, and their husbands found them. Silently, they too dropped to their knees.

And then, footsteps muted by the snow, Clint burst through the door with a whoop. Courtney with an audible cry of "Forgive the interruption, Lord!" sprang into his arms, sure that her feet never once touched the floor.

Only then did the women cry. Even Cousin Bella blew her nose on a dainty handkerchief before scolding Doc George for not wearing heavier clothing.

"Are you frozen, my darling? Doc George must check you for frostbite. Oh, Clint, Clint, you're safe—what about Efraim—and John—and did everybody get home all right?"

Courtney's words poured out senselessly. But Clint understood, his rich laugh assured her. " 'All's well that ends well,' as Donolar would say. We men are fit as fiddles—just lonesome," he whispered the last phrase as he kissed her ear. "But what on earth is all this?"

Then everybody was talking at once. Children, undisciplined, were looping their popcorn strings on the tree in wild abandon. And Mandy, singing lustily, was bringing in the midnight feast.

The clock struck 11. And the cuckoo clock, sounding hoarse to Courtney's ears, mimicked the call. Weary of their toys and exhausted from their new freedom, little heads began to droop.

"Bedtime!" Cousin Bella's no-nonsense announcement met with no protests. And in the hour that followed, every spare room in the house was spread with pallets. Their parents would occupy the freshly made beds, Cousin Bella promised. Only it did not come out even as she had planned. There was nothing to do but put a few of the leftover cherubs on the beds she, Clint, and Courtney occupied. Maybe a reshuffling could be made later, she said vaguely and then looked a little embarrassed.

It made little difference because the grandfather clock and the cuckoo clock (having, miracle of miracles, found renewed energy and caught up with its elder) pealed out the mystical hour of midnight. It was Christmas Day!

"Merry Christmas, my darling!" Clint's arms folded tenderly around his bride. But not before she saw the deep ravines of fatigue in his pale face. He *must* get some sleep.

But how? "There must be a prayer of thanksgiving!" Brother Jim boomed. And then there were carols to sing . . .

Courtney was too exhausted to note that the storm had ended as abruptly as it began when, as the gray dawn came, she and Clint wearily climbed the stairs. "My quarters—" he mumbled as if talking in his sleep.

Inside his bedroom, a lamp glowed softly to reveal countless children bunched in sleep. "We'll go to my room, darling," Courtney whispered. "Anywhere—just so I can get my shoes off—"

A dying fire made a pale glow in Courtney's room. Enough for Courtney to see that two of the Laughten children lay across her own bed. She managed to ease John Henry over enough that she could squeeze the blanketed baby close to his warm, little body.

"Muvver?" John Henry's muffled voice wanted to know.

"Mother's here," Courtney whispered and patted him softly while looking hopelessly at her husband. Together, they laughed. Then he stretched out beside the sleeping children and patted a place beside him in invitation.

It took Courtney some time to unbutton her shoes. The shoebuttoner kept hooking around the pearl buttons, making it difficult for her tired fingers to remove it. She should change her clothes, but she was too frustrated and fatigued to care. Besides the room had grown chill.

Numbly, she slipped into bed, easing her body crosswise in the narrow space remaining between Clint and the footboard, trying not to awaken him as she pulled the covers around her shivering body. "Court-ney?" he mumbled from his maze of slumber, his voice sounding much like John Henry's.

She reassured him in like manner. "I'm here," she said softly.

Clint reached for and found her hand. "—love you—will you m-mar-ry—me?"

Courtney snuggled closer. "I did," she giggled.

Someday, she thought dreamily, she would tell him of his proposal to a married woman! Someday together they would review their strange wedding night. Someday (she yawned and stretched luxuriously) they would recall this—their first night alone and yet not alone at all—in "a tumultuous privacy of storm." And some-day . . .

Then, surrendering to the giant of weariness, obe-diently Courtney Desmond let the warm hand holding hers draw her into his world of sleep . . .

*   *   *

"Ah, yes, th' weddin'! 'Twas th' grandest ever. An' th' shindig that follored . . . now we're here t'tell you that was the strangest part of all," settlers would say myste-riously as the eyes of the next generation grew wide with wonder.

The wistful children and their children's children would listen. And, like others throughout the ages, they would sigh in resignation at never being able to witness anything quite so splendid as Grandpa and Grandma in the Pioneer Days.

CHAPTER 16
Elopement

She must have dozed, Courtney thought fuzzily, as she did not hear Clint leave the room. She remembered that he had been there, but the rest of the world seemed topsy-turvy. Why, even the Laughten children were gone!

Quickly, she pulled herself up on one elbow and felt for her robe—only to realize that she needed none. She was still fully dressed! And one look in the mirror caused her to groan in despair. Look at her hair! And the beautiful going-away suit was rumpled and covered with lint that clung tenaciously to the pleated skirt. Of course . . . stuffing from the rag dolls. Where *was* everybody?

With cold fingers, she drew the front drapes partly open and gasped. Overhead was an improbably blue, blue Christmas sky. The late-rising winter sun blinked a sleepy red eye, then sparkled brilliantly on the snow, reflecting a kaleidoscope of sparkling color to rival the world's most expensive diamonds. A very good omen. As was the tantalizing odor of coffee drifting up the stairs.

A soft knock broke into her thoughts. "Courtney?" Clint whispered, opening the door a crack.

"Don't come in! I'm not dressed!"

"*Sh-h-h-h!* That's the general idea—"

"Clint—don't you *dare*!" Courtney whispered back fiercely.

"Be quiet, darling. The others are sleeping—except Mandy. She's in on the scheme—"

"What scheme?" Courtney's voice was doubtful, but she found herself inching toward the door where Clint was handing her something—*what on earth?*

"Put these on—and hurry or it won't work!"

"I don't know what you're talking about—and you don't mean—you *can't* mean I'm to wear *pants?*"

Clint's laugh was low. "They're mine—the best I could come up with. Certainly you can't walk in those silly shoes women wear. Put on your boots and pull these trousers on over a skirt—we're going to *elope!*"

Courtney, her teeth chattering, laughed in spite of herself. What a comical scene! The house crowded with bodies . . . the newlyweds, husband and wife in name only, conspiring to run away . . . with the bride clad in her husband's clothes! And she had thought *she* was the romantic?

Taking the pants gingerly, Courtney ran an experimental foot into one leg, almost tripped, then—casting a suspicious eye at the door—tugged at the other leg. All the while, Clint was depositing a mountain of woolen shirts, mittens, and scarves beside a heavy plaid mackinaw.

In the midst of buttoning the scratchy shirt over her blouse, Courtney came to her senses. Why, what Clint was proposing was impossible. They could not be seen like this, even if it were proper to leave the guests . . . and go to a fine hotel with her stuffed like a strutting pigeon?

"Clint—we can't!"

"We can—and we will! Are you dressed yet?"

"No, but," she promised rashly, secretly feeling a rising excitement, "I'll meet you downstairs in five minutes!"

Whatever Clint's wild plan was, she—his wife—was a part of it. *His wife!* At the thought, her heart became intoxicated—skimming over the snow like a bobsled racing downhill—totally out of control and not caring!

An excited Courtney paused only for a moment to inspect herself in the triple mirror. The light was better now and she had a good view of black hair tumbling to her waist, dark eyes sparkling, lips made scarlet by health in spite of what Doc George thought of her slight being, and cheeks flushed with anticipation.

But the rest of her—my goodness, the doctor should see her rotund body now with its layer after layer of clothing. She had a good laugh then hurried to pack a blue flannel nightie and matching robe into a paisley bag. Her hair brush . . . a bar of lilac-scented soap . . . and, oh yes, the journal, her wedding gift to Clint. Not much of a trousseau, but it would have to do.

The rest of the house was still dark, drapes drawn against the light. A grinning Mandy motioned Courtney into the warmth of the kitchen. Clint entered from the back door at the same time, stamping snow from his boots. He inspected Courtney, suppressing a smile, then drew her to him in a bear hug that shut off her breath and all recriminations.

"Drank yore coffee, child'run, else de nosey Miz Rueben's bound bein' in heah—den yore plans iz spilt beans!"

Their plans? Their plans, Clint told her quickly, were to hike out the back way to the main road. But how? The temperature had dropped as the men came home last night, causing a silver thaw. Roads were frozen over—leaving a trail where he, Doc George, and Efraim had come home last night. Bridge was still intact. Wagons could cross. Doc George had tried it already. Then why weren't they taking the buggy? Too noisy . . . Cousin Bella might need it . . . and not grand enough for his bride.

"You mean we're *walking* all the way—like *this*? How far?" Courtney gasped, almost choking on the hot coffee.

"Now, don' y'all go worryin' dat purty head, Miz Courtney hon, Mistah Clint gonna be takin' awful good care.

He dun sent Mr. Efraim on de hoss an' Mistah Efraim he gonna meet y'all at de main road wid ah survice car'age!"

Clint nodded. " 'Dat's right," he whispered in Courtney's ear, then in a normal tone, "Thank you, Mandy—finish your coffee, Courtney. As for clothes, darling, I'll purchase you the prettiest dress Madam Monique has stitched!"

ONE, TWO, THREE . . . the grandfather clock grumbled.

One, two, three, four . . . cuck-oo, cuck-oo . . .

"Come, that would wake the dead!" Clint pulled Courtney to her feet.

And Mandy pushed her back down.

"Git dat pic'anick baskit, Mistah Clint—whilst Miz Courtney heah writes de note—"

The note? Courtney took the pencil but looked blankly into Mandy's laughing, black eyes.

"Y'all cain't be thankin' uv runnin' away wid no note—would'n be no 'lopement a-tall—"

Courtney stifled a laugh. "Well, now, we wouldn't want to make a social blunder, would we? This wedding having gone so perfectly so far!"

Quickly, she printed a note and handed it to Mandy. "You can read now, Mandy—surprise them all with the words!"

Laughing and radiant, the newlyweds hurried out the back door as the cook was left pondering over the words:

GONE TO "INNISFREE"—AND BEYOND!
THANK YOU FOR EVERYTHING, BUT DO NOT
TRY TO FIND US. WE ARE HONEYMOONING,
REMEMBER?
OUR LOVE AND GOD'S BLESSINGS,

                THE HAPPIEST PAIR IN
                THE WORLD!

CHAPTER 17
A New Identity

They walked hand-in-hand over the frozen snow, winding among the fir, pine, and spruce trees. Some of the drooping trees were packaged with snow. Others were decorated with Christmas ornaments—long, glistening spikes of ice.

Over and over Clint asked if Courtney was warm enough. And over and over she nodded in wordless appreciation. How could she be cold when her heart glowed with an inner fire of sheer joy? Let others have their "civilized country." Courtney would not exchange this day in the "wilderness," as Mother called it, for a tropical honeymoon.

No, she thought determinedly, she was not going to think about Mother. Not now. This day belonged to Clint.

They came out of the woods unexpectedly. And there (*Praise the Lord!*) was Efraim in the promised service carriage, courtesy of Ma Becker's *Chateau*. Efraim teased her about her garb as Clint helped her into the carriage. Then, tucking a robe about her feet, the two men talked over her head. Courtney heard little except Efraim's telling Clint that his partner, Robert VanKoten, had—at his invitation—attended the wedding, although he was unable to stay for the reception as his daughter had an engagement and felt they should return.

That reminded Courtney to inquire, "I didn't see Horace. Was he there?"

Efraim laughed. "You two had eyes only for each other."

"True." Did she only imagine that Clint's voice sounded strained? Well, she was not going to worry about that either. She was simply going to revel in the moment.

Why, then, did she turn as they topped a rise at the bend in the road leading back to the city, to look over her shoulder in the general direction of Gambling Gate? She would be unable to pick it out from the drifts of snow.

But she did! And there, sure enough, was a thin column of smoke curling from the falling-down chimney. Courtney opened her mouth in dismay. Then, just as quickly, she closed it. Nothing was going to spoil this day . . .

* * *

Ma Becker's *Chateau*'s rather grand interior denied the weather-beaten exterior. It must be very old, as time in the Pacific Northwest was measured, as it spoke of architects who wanted the best of the two worlds. People who wanted to conquer the wild frontier while at the same time maintaining their Eastern plush and privacy. Chandeliers. Velvet upholstery, once red but now shading into rose and creases of pink, where—Courtney suspected—overweight drummers had sunk deep to exchange harrowing experiences along their trails. Deep carpet—were the rugs really Persian?—softened every footfall. Something about the place whispered peace. A perfect haven for the wonderful three days ahead in which two lives would be enjoined forever in actuality.

Courtney left Clint and Efraim in the lobby and, relieved that she had been undetected, unlocked their suite. Here, too, was that certain grandeur. But she must not spend time in admiration. Clint was taking her shopping so she would be presentable at dinner. The two of them could explore tonight . . . *tonight* . . .

Courtney's heart gave an extra pump as quickly she stripped off the heavy outer garments and tried desperately to smooth the wrinkles from her suit. At best, she looked like something from a missionary barrel. Thank goodness for the color in her cheeks, and it was a double plus that Clint liked her cloud of dark hair hanging loose. So she walked with newfound dignity down the stairs to meet him.

Madam Monique was as French as her name. With an eye for business, the petite seamstress darted around her prospective customer in bird-like fashion. Inspecting her. Sizing her up through narrowed blue-green eyes. All the while her upswept hair with its mass of frizzy curls (made red by Old World henna plant undeniably) kept bouncing up and down in delight.

"Ah-h-h, yees, nasturtium eez right color—right for fall, yees? No chape, chape rates, but—right!"

While Madam Monique was behind a beaded curtain, Courtney, wondering if the woman lived up to the fine reputation Clint had given her as a seamstress, allowed her eyes to wander around the cologne-scented dressing room. The decor jolted the senses. The furniture, in contrast to its owner, was overstuffed. The walls were draped with chintzes that ran wild. Butterflies and birds met in midair and collided where seams were unmatched. If her clothes looked like *this* . . .

But they did not. Several minutes later, Courtney went into the adjoining room where Clint waited. His gasp of admiration told her exactly what she had decided already. The color—nasturtium (burnt-orange, Madam Monique had confided)—brought added color to her cheeks and turned her flawless complexion to Dresden china. And, Courtney admitted modestly to herself, the color was certainly a foil for her black hair.

"Nasturtium?" Clint shook his head doubtfully as Madam Monique explained with flamboyant gestures. "My wife looks more like a tulip."

Adoration showed in his face and his fingers were an undisguised caress as he touched the petaled ecru jabot that cupped Courtney's face.

Whatever the price, it was worth it. There were some other purchases. A coat. The right shoes. And some (*ahem*) —well—personal things—lingerie—the *right* things for a bride, he understood, yes? Clint seemed to be paying no attention, just the bill. And Courtney's mind had stuck like a broken record on the music machine. *My wife* . . .

Clint steered her quickly past the saloon where rubbery-legged patrons staggered out and gaped openly at so grand a lady passing their way. And soon the two of them were away from the business houses and back in the solitude of their postcard world. The snow was still undisturbed at the edge of town except where the two of them had forged steps leading to the hotel. The air was fresh and pure. Courtney filled her lungs gratefully. Then, seized by a sudden coltish desire, she let go of Clint's hand and romped ahead.

Bending over, she scooped up a double handful of snow and formed a giant snowball. Turning to Clint, she commanded, "Surrender!"

"Never!" And two giant steps brought him to her. "Do you know what happens to such warlike women?"

Not waiting for an answer, Clint grabbed her teasingly. Then, looking into her upturned face, he groaned and bent to kiss her.

"This is where I belong," she whispered. "This is what I have waited for all my life—this—"

"Oh, my darling, yes, *yes*, YES!"

Reluctantly, he let her go. "Hark, the dark!" He smiled with an effort. "And time to dine!"

"Why, Mr. Desmond, marriage has made you into a poet. You—"

But she was unable to finish the thought. They were no longer alone. They were being watched!

"What's wrong, sweetheart?"

"N-nothing—I'm just c-cold." Courtney tried a normal voice. What she wanted to blurt out was that she had seen a face—the face of Milton Bellevue.

"Let's get you inside," Clint said with concern as they turned back toward the *Chateau.*

Courtney told herself that she was wrong. That Milton Bellevue was in jail. And the face could belong to anybody. She must not allow imagination to spoil these 72 hours. She would savor every moment of her new identity.

And she kept the promise to herself, her heart bursting with pride when Clint told the waiter that Mrs. Desmond would like French pastry for dessert. *Mrs. Desmond!*

It was as Mrs. Desmond that Courtney willingly went into her husband's arms a short time later in the privacy of their suite. And it was as Mrs. Desmond that she pulled his head down to meet her waiting lips.

"My darling little madonna," Clint whispered. "Our marriage got off to a strange start. And we do not know what the end will be . . . but in between is a beautiful love story . . ."

CHAPTER 18
Fulfillment

Mr. and Mrs. Clinton Desmond returned to Mansion-in-the-Wild, their eyes alive with wonder. They looked so happy, valley folk said. So in love. In love with one another, but in love with life as well. Courtney, still walking on the misty cloud of her new role, lived in the present tense with no concept of what life was soon—very soon—to become.

"Oh yes, our time in the city was wonderful," Courtney breathed happily to Cousin Bella. "Wonderful and every bit as romantic as the note we left!"

"Naughty children," Cousin Bella said with a faraway smile. "Tell me all about it."

The two of them were supervising the moving of Courtney's personal things into Clint's bedroom. Cousin Bella offered the entire upstairs. Courtney declined. More room, she said significantly, could come when there were three of them instead of two.

"Hang onto it, my dear—hang onto your happiness with both hands."

"I have and I will!" Courtney promised with stars in her eyes.

Those innocent stars continued to twinkle as she shared with Cousin Bella the grandeur of the *Chateau*, Madam Monique's tactics, and the stores that now offered bolts of linen and chintz, rolls of velvet, and jeweled braiding. The fishermen had brought in fresh crabs. Oh, so good! And would Cousin Bella believe that the sketches Lance had left on consignment at the fish-house were sold? The city was spreading out, everyone had said, and trains were running more regularly now. Lots of ships bringing imports from China—the sweetest hand-painted wooden toys . . .

Courtney, her heart suffused in happiness, remembered the tenderness with which Clint had looked at her when she examined the toys . . . china doll for a girl . . . train engine for a boy.

Toward the end, there had been no need for talking. She and Clint simply walked together, silent in their common dream. Savoring the memory of her shy suggestion that "it might happen sooner than we plan . . ."

Courtney forced herself to come back to earth by asking how everything had gone here during their absence.

Cousin Bella frowned. "Frankly, I am a little bewildered at Donolar's reports. He probably imagined his sightings—lights and smoke—over there—"

"Over there" meant Gambling Gate—words Cousin Bella found distasteful. "Maybe he didn't imagine it," Courtney said without intending to verify Donolar's reports.

Cousin Bella's head jerked erect. "I think," she said as if the decision were not new, "we had best have Efraim here to do some investigating. We will include that Mr. VanKoten—where shall I hang this dress?"

*   *   *

Clint returned to the mines. And Courtney resumed her visits with the valley folk—dividing her time equally between Doc George and Brother Jim.

Coyly, she gathered all the information she could from the doctor concerning body and behavioral changes expectant mothers would undergo. And how should they care for themselves for the welfare of both mother and child?

"Mighty good of you to take such interest in our patients." Doc George smoothed his muttonchops, making the line disappear where the side-whiskers met the meticulously trimmed white beard. Then glancing at her sideways, he said slyly, "Since you're that interested in the field of homeopathic medicine—"

The pause called for a nod. Courtney obliged.

"Well, calcium for the bones—lots of rich cow's milk is a must in the diet. A variety of fresh vegetables and fruits which grow so abundantly here. And, as you know, no purgative compounds such as calomel—softens the gums—could cause the teeth to fall out. Have to teach our patients to avoid these medicine shows where quacks and scoundrels promote the use of quack prescriptions —herbs claimed to cure everything from coyote bite to dropsy. And," he chuckled, "no need for ipecac to induce vomiting—nature takes care of that!"

How well she knew. Courtney had watched every move her friend made as he ministered to women who felt for sure their plight was "Eve's curse" and helped him reassure them that it was all worthwhile. Doc George was a real boon in the valley, serving as he did and scoffing at his "greedy colleagues—parasites in the flesh—who charged a dollar just for staying overnight when a woman is due to deliver."

"We all appreciate you," she said warmly.

Doc George beamed and his blush deepened like that of a proper Santa Claus. "No halo for this white head, dear child, but if you're that interested—well, I have a book, a recent edition, mind you, called *Prenatal Care*."

"I would appreciate it," Courtney assured him and turned away before seeing the knowing look he cast her direction.

He halted the team and applied the brake. And squeals of joy from countless children announced to whoever the next patient was that "th' doc 'n Miz Courtney Ma'm wuz a-comin!"

Courtney smiled in fulfillment. *Almost . . .*

CHAPTER 19
Company for Dinner

The night Efraim brought his partner, Robert Van-Koten, and his daughter, Roberta, to dinner was both revealing and secretive, Courtney thought in review. Cousin Bella extended the invitation well in advance. It included a suggestion that the guests would be welcome for an overnight stay, the distance being too great for traveling back.

"And," she added to Courtney, "a bit unsafe as well. I dislike having anybody who is unfamiliar with this part of the world toying with the darkness. By the way, dear, has Donolar spoken further of his—er—sightings?"

"No, Cousin Bella."

It was true. Although Donolar had dogged her every footstep since she and Clint returned from their honeymoon—could they have been married a month!—he had made no mention of Gambling Gate. Not that she had encouraged him, Courtney thought with a shiver. The place both fascinated and repelled her. She wondered fleetingly just why her cousin wished to talk with Efraim concerning the property. Oh well, it was unlikely that the topic would come up when guests were present. Or was it? Mr. VanKoten was Efraim's partner and—

Determinedly, Courtney concentrated on the menu. Mandy welcomed suggestions, she said, when there "wuz city fo'ks a-comin'." Mrs. Rueben was making dust fly all directions in a frenzied effort to "spic-and-span der house." Mandy declared that the housekeeper would be sweeping the chimneys out before the big night. Donolar puzzled over the centerpiece. And Cousin Bella said she hoped there would be no late-January storm to close the road.

There wasn't. A Chinook wind melted away the snow gently without creating a flood. And the evening of the VanKotens' arrival was mild with only a silver mist of rain.

Courtney was dressing when the small party arrived. She had chosen a pine-green silk dress that fell into soft folds like a caress around her ankles just before touching the floor. She was brushing her dark hair until it gleamed when Clint rapped then burst through the door. There he stopped.

"You look like something that just stepped out of a dream," he breathed. "*My* dream!"

Courtney rushed to him in welcome. "Then let me step right back in—oh, Clint, the time—"

"Ah, yes, the time. I should have stopped the clocks! But please, Ma'm, I prithee, just one kiss—"

"*Just* one!" Courtney cautioned, but it was Clint who pulled away. Laughing at how weak her legs went each time her husband of four weeks touched her, Courtney hurried to lay out his dark suit and the white shirt Mandy had starched and ironed just hours before.

Clint opened his bureau drawer for a shoe brush. "Oh, Courtney—I can't believe this—I—why, I must ask your forgiveness and God's understanding—"

"What on earth—"

"I failed to give you the wedding gift I had planned!"

Courtney laughed merrily, concerns of the day forgotten. "Efraim said we had eyes only for each other. I believe him! You see, darling, I forgot, too." She took the carefully written journal from her writing desk. "My very personal thoughts—my heart—"

Clint opened it, glanced eagerly at the first entry, and said softly, "I shall treasure this forever—reading it over and over."

"I will add to it," Courtney promised mistily, "as—well—as things happen—"

Clint looked at her quizzically. Courtney did not meet his gaze but accepted the tiny Bible encased in rich velure—the perfect gift for a God-loving bride. "Oh, Clint—"

The hallway clock interrupted the moment with a throaty gong. Without waiting for the cuckoo clock to echo the warning, Cousin Bella rang the silver bell.

Springing apart like two guilty children, the young Desmonds assumed an air of dignity and descended the stairs . . .

*   *   *

Cousin Bella took special care with her appearance that evening. In a departure from the stark black and white, she wore a wide lavender-blue velvet ribbon about her neck, pinned in front with her mother's quaint cameo. Her eyes seemed to sparkle when she introduced the visitors.

"The rest of us have met," she addressed Clint and Courtney as they entered the dining room, "and so it is my pleasure to present Mr. Robert VanKoten—"

She paused as Mr. VanKoten came forward and bowed gravely. Courtney judged him to be past 50 and noted his impeccable dress. There was a certain elegance in his manner, a natural charm that his little goatee, lively dark eyes, and luxuriant near-black hair reflected.

"Ah, madame, how lovely you are—like a flower a--bloom in the desert."

Courtney found herself curtsying, a small gesture of finishing school she had thought forgotten.

"—*and*," Cousin broke in pointedly, "his daughter, Miss Roberta."

Courtney's eyes met Roberta's with a start. The girl, totally unlike her father, was far too tall and much too thin. She stooped slightly in an apparent effort to conceal her height. Her amber-brown eyes, looking out of place in the thin face, were her best feature. But the eyes looked frightened and so desperately shy. Courtney hoped that the hand she extended to Roberta was warm and reassuring.

"It is so nice to have someone so near my own age to talk with, Miss VanKoten."

"Call me Roberta—please do."

"Indeed I will, and you are to call me Courtney. Cousin Bella, I hope you have seated Roberta near me."

"Unfortunately, no—the men outnumbering us greatly, as is the general picture here in the Northwest. Efraim, if you will seat the lady between you and Donolar—"

Talk flowed easily. Robert VanKoten was a delightful conversationalist. Surely, Courtney thought in fascination, he had been everywhere and seen everything. Roberta's mother had died giving birth to their only child. ("That was in Paris, you know, where we remained while I handled the legal affairs of the *Fleur* Perfumery ere coming West.") That explained his knowledge of flowers, which so delighted Donolar—perhaps even by a stretch of the imagination, his identification of other plants. But birds? And he discussed the arts knowledgeably, saying it was he who purchased Lance's paintings! Certainly, the man must be an avid reader because, again to Donolar's delight, he peppered his speech generously with quotes from Shakespeare.

Roberta remained quiet, speaking only when spoken to, in spite of Efraim's gallant attempts to draw her into the conversation. Small wonder, Courtney reflected sadly, that her brother was less than charmed. Even the silk suit she wore, obviously expensive, hung on her sparse frame much like a garment drooping from its hanger. And yet there was something about her that appealed to Courtney. A sort of identification. A feeling that behind the lackluster exterior lurked a fine mind. And more. A need . . .

Over coffee in the library, Cousin Bella steered the conversation with practiced skill to another vein.

Did Mr. VanKoten like this part of the world? Surely it must be quite a change.

"Quite a change—a pleasant one—though challenging."

"Then you think you will be staying?" Cousin Bella's question was almost blunt.

Mr. VanKoten looked a little surprised. "Oh, yes—I had rather thought your nephew told you."

"Clint doesn't know, Mr. VanKoten," Efraim said. "He is the nephew. I am a cousin—as are Clint's wife, my sister Courtney, and our brother, Donolar."

"Ah yes, so you told me," Mr. VanKoten said graciously. "How could I have forgotten? And there is another sister, I believe—and your mother?"

Courtney wondered fleetingly what family relationships had to do with the VanKotens' plans. She waited for the next words.

"The Bellevues are related to both Mr. Desmond—may I call you Clint?—and my young partner's family. Correct?"

It was Efraim who explained the relationships quickly. As he did so, Courtney observed that all eyes were turned to the guests expectantly.

"Then you knew they escaped—"

"The *brothers!*" Donolar's cry of alarm cut through the politely quiet atmosphere like a knife. "I knew—I saw—they will kill my butterflies—and *us*—oh—"

"It's all right, Donolar!" Clint's voice had an edge and his eyes on Mr. VanKoten held a warning.

"Yes, son, if there's a problem, we will solve it, rest assured!" Doc George boomed.

"Amen!" said Brother Jim, doubling his fists.

Obviously flustered, Mr. VanKoten murmured apologies. Roberta's face was chalky. "Perhaps, Father, we should—take our leave," she ventured timidly.

"Not at all!" Arabella Kennedy was back in charge. "You have touched a nerve, but all the more reason we need to talk. Efraim, is there an explanation?"

Efraim's nostrils flared slightly. "Yes—although I had planned it at another time. The breakout well may make a difference—but, well, hang it all, VanKoten, there may be a conflict of interests here. As a fledgling Christian, I feel—well, I may have to step out of the case—"

CHAPTER 20
The Balm of Understanding

Roberta VanKoten looked haggard as the evening wore on and complained privately to Courtney of a headache. Courtney made their polite excuses and left the men to talk with Cousin Bella.

"I will show you to your quarters, Roberta. You are to occupy the room that was mine before my marriage."

Roberta nodded without comment. But, once they were alone in the upstairs bedroom where Mrs. Rueben and Mandy had thoughtfully laid a fire and turned back the covers for the guest, the girl seemed to change completely.

"The room is beautiful, Courtney—like you," she breathed in admiration.

Courtney laughed. "I never thought of myself as beautiful at all—at least, not until I saw myself reflected in Clint's eyes."

Roberta sighed. "It must be wonderful—being in love—something I have never experienced and never expect to. I accepted myself long ago for what I am—unattractive, a disappointment to my father—"

"Oh, come, come!" Courtney scolded gently as she turned up the wick on the lamp to flood the room with mellow light. "Aren't you being hard on yourself?"

"Maybe, but life has made me that way." Roberta's voice was bitter. "My mother was a beautiful woman and you can see for yourself that my father is handsome and charming. My chromosomes must date back to the potato-digging Irish whose genes we carry—and without comment! Even my gender was a disappointment—supposed to be a boy, you know—hence, *Roberta*—" Roberta stopped, aghast at her own words. "Forgive me—I don't usually carry on like this, particularly to strangers."

Courtney reached out to touch the thin hand. "Perhaps," she said softly, "because you sensed a kindred spirit. It is strange how God sends understanding people our way. Did you take note of the ancestral lineup in the library?"

"The Bellevues and the Glamoras?"

Courtney lifted her face to face Roberta's in surprise. "You knew the names?"

Roberta's laugh was a little bitter. "Oh yes, my father's mind, you know. He researched the names while practicing in Philadelphia where I was attempting some law courses—not too successfully, I'm afraid. I could master the work, but I could not do battle with a man's world. Men like beauty but not brains—oh, you will forgive me, Courtney—I—I—"

"It's quite all right, but you may find it different here. Or perhaps you have already. The Columbia Valley settlers accept people as they are. But I am puzzled as to why Mr. VanKoten was so interested in my ancestors. Do you mind my asking?"

It occurred to Courtney that the two of them had been standing in the middle of the bedroom and she had not invited her guest to hang up her heavy coat. But Roberta's answer might clear up some niggling questions, so she brushed good manners aside as she waited.

"You have a right to know. I personally see no sense to all the secrecy. My father also knew the Worthingtons and the Villards—the Villards of the railroad, you know?"

Yes, Courtney knew.

He wanted Rambling Gate. Came West to get it. Sent her ahead as a scout, in fact—as well as looking after three other parcels of land he had acquired.

Then, the girl was far from being stupid, Courtney realized. She had a keen mind. What was to be further admired, Roberta was open, uncomplicated, and thoroughly enjoyable.

"The whole matter would have been so simple had there not been a previous bid—your cousin's—and—"

"Cousin Bella!" Courtney gasped. "She wants Gambling Gate? I can't believe it—Roberta, have you seen the place?"

"Only pictures—sketches—and it looks a little ghastly."

"*Ghostly!* If you would remain as my guest, we could explore it from a distance—although it is declared off-limits for me by my family. But two of us together?"

"You are a dear person, Courtney. I should like that, but Father needs me to help resolve the purchase. May I have a rain check? I admired you so much at the church and was too shy to—to bother you—but now that we are friends?"

"Friends indeed, my dear Roberta—providing you forgive me for my breaches of etiquette—hang your coat here." Courtney opened the large chifforobe. "And there are towels here in the closet. Use the desk or the vanity—anything you wish."

As the two of them made Roberta comfortable, a million questions crisscrossed in Courtney's mind. She was glad when Roberta invited her to stay for a time.

"But your headache?" Courtney asked hesitantly.

Roberta waved a thin hand. "Gone—and I want to talk. About Rambling Gate, your cousin wanted you and your husband to have possession as a wedding gift. My father has paid money down—and yet her bid was lower. And now it seems that neither of them may be the owner with the Bellevues on the loose—it's like a game of cat-and-dead-mouse!"

"They have no claim, Clint says. Efraim would know."

"No claim, but Alexis is tied in somehow and, clever as the woman is, she seems to be putty in the hands of a man. I have a feeling that my father and your cousin may become allies before the night is over—even though your brother refuses to help either."

"Can you understand his position?"

"I can—and a lot more—I—" Roberta blushed. "I—well, understand your brother—and, oh, Courtney, I wish I were beautiful!"

"Wait until your week with me is over!" Courtney smiled.

CHAPTER 21
Foreboding

Brief February passed. It entered with a soft sift of snow, then erased it in exit. A mild winter, farmers said, a little too mild. Could do the winter wheat in. Or could mean a late blizzard, sudden thaw, floods . . .

Courtney scarcely heard their dire predictions. The honeymoon had lasted "su'prisin'ly long, *reely* in love, them two," women murmured among themselves in envy. But it was no surprise to Courtney. Love like theirs would endure forever . . . come drought . . . come flood . . . come whatever the elements had to offer. So she smiled smugly, even managing to put her own concerns in the background.

But the uncertainties of the world are always out there, she was to remember later—out there just waiting for a subject to light upon. For now, secure in her life here and the great love which bound her to Clint, Courtney was sure she could cope. It was as Brother Jim said, "We can outwit fear by fighting fire with fire! Look it in the face! Admit it, accept it—then deal with it mightily!"

Clint was spending more time at the mines. But Courtney understood. Besides, Courtney told him a little too brightly, there was so much to *do*! Letters to write (she must write to Lance again as there had been no answer when she wrote Mother all about the wedding). Talks with Cousin Bella (there had been no further mention of the property in dispute and Courtney wanted to have a talk with her cousin). And her reading (catching up with Donolar on the classics, helping Mandy to further her reading the Bible and, yes, she would begin some simple lessons for Mrs. Rueben now that she was understanding English instruction). All these were secret thoughts to enter in her diary. And most secret of all was her reading the book Doc George had found, *Prenatal Care*. One of the fundamentals was exercise. So she must ride more . . . walk more . . . neither which she would speak of except to Donolar. The others were such worriers! It was undoubtedly safe for her to venture farther than they allowed. And certainly she needed to be busy in order to ease her loneliness for Clint—and, admittedly, her concerns for his safety. If the Bellevues *were* in these parts . . .

Nonsense! They wouldn't dare. Escapees would be miles away.

And then Courtney's serenity was broken. It was as if someone had disturbed placid waters by dropping two heavy stones into an unsuspecting pond. Which, in a very real sense, was what happened.

On a blustery day in March Courtney overheard Mrs. Rueben declare that it was time for spring cleaning. "I begun a'ready—strippin' de beds, airin' de quilts— Scriptahs dun been sayin' 'Considah de ant, thou sluggahd, considah huh ways 'n be wise'!" Mandy said pointedly.

Courtney smiled before closing her bedroom door. A harmonious beginning was the best beginning for her prayer. And the housekeeper's words to the cook were apt to be less than harmonious. "My voice shalt thou hear in the morning, O Lord . . ." she copied from the psalm in her journal.

Prayers said, Courtney wrote a hasty note to Lance telling of her concern for her mother. She was about to seal the envelope when she remembered that Robert VanKoten had purchased Lance's paintings. Lance must know about that.

Cousin Bella was going to the fort for supplies and would post the letter, she said. And no, Donolar need not drive her. George Washington had some business to attend to—something about a new approach to birthing. Wasn't he showing a lively interest in the matter of late?

Wishing to divert Cousin Bella, Courtney approached the topic of Rambling Gate. "I hadn't known of your interest in the property—well, adjoining your estate," she began.

Cousin Bella gave a rare sigh. "How black-and-white you women below 40 see life." Her voice stretched far away. "Once George Washington and I promised to stay together for life—like you and Clint—then *she*—" Arabella Kennedy's voice was half statement, half plea. "Try to understand, my dear, that some things never change— that I am first a woman and then Clint's aunt and your cousin."

"I have known that since our talk—when you confided about you and Doc George. I have seen you in a new light since then—but I don't see—"

"What one has to do with the other? As a woman, I guess I wanted the property of that Villard woman who married the man to whom I was betrothed—meaning that, as your concerned relative, I did not wish something like that to happen to the two of you! I somehow equated the two. Alexis is still trying to gain possession—and I don't want her near! There I've done it again—talked too much."

"Oh no, dear Cousin Bella. I understand—at least, I think I do. But Clint and I do not need Rambling Gate to hold our love together."

"And neither do George Washington and I—*now*. But never let anything or anybody come between you—waiting until you are past 50 to put the shattered bones of your love together—oh, there's George Washington! But," she said slowly, "I may—just *may*, mind you—tell him today that I am willing to forget the past—that place *over there*—letting Robert VanKoten have it, lest this become a battle similar to the Bellevues and the Glamoras, which one day it might. I—well, please do not think me a doddering idiot when I say that the time has come for me to accept the past."

Did she mean—*could* Cousin Bella mean—that she had loved and lost only to regain? That she was ready to love again?

Courtney longed to embrace her cousin. But Arabella Kennedy's guard was up. Doc George had rapped impatiently on the door with his never-applied whip. And Courtney saw a flicker of tenderness in Cousin Bella's eyes.

* * *

That afternoon Cousin Bella brought Courtney a letter from Lance. The letter was the first stone. The Lady Ana had declared herself unable to read details of her "poor baby's unfortunate marriage." Lance, although he felt himself invading Courtney's privacy and begged her forgiveness, read the letter aloud whereupon her mother had gone into a swoon and refused to be aroused. The doctor said she should not be alone. And how soon did Courtney think weather would permit the promised visit?

Courtney wept, laying the letter aside at that point. Her burden of guilt was back. Followed by a certain rebellion. And then despair. As usual, Mother was controlling her life even from a distance.

But she and Clint *had* promised. A promise was a sacred thing. They must go. And yet what could they do to liven her days? Clint belonged *here*. And she could not bear to allow him to leave her *there*. Another trap was closing in about her. Did her marriage count for nothing to Mother? And what about the family she hoped to start?

At length, Courtney dried her eyes and read the remainder of Lance's letter.

> Discouragement, like a wedge, seems driven into dear Lady Ana's heart. The doctors wonder if her deep depression results from any physical malady. Forgive me when I say that your mother never learned to control her emotions. She feels abandoned since Vanessa married. You knew your sister had given birth to twins? She remains in London.

So Vanessa was married! What was more, she was the mother of twins! Courtney's shock was born less of the news than of Mother's lack of happiness for her favorite child.

Dear Lance. He went on to say that he tried in vain to convince Lady Ana that the sun "had its sinking spells" too, but it always rose each morning. He would do the best he could for her. Until Courtney and Clint came. And yes, he was looking forward greatly to their arrival.

The letter left Courtney restless and depressed. She doubted if the weather was dependable enough for the long journey over the Continental Divide. Efraim would find out . . . and Clint would keep his word . . . but meantime, she would invite Roberta for a visit. It seemed important.

And then stone two! In need of a bit of air, Courtney left the house quietly and crossed the bridge leading to the Isle of Innisfree. "Yoo-hoo, Donolar?"

Her brother's tortured face peered cautiously from his cabin window. Wordlessly, he pointed toward Rambling Gate. And from the chimney came wisps of smoke . . .

CHAPTER 22
Searching

Everyone seemed so rushed these days. Courtney found herself wondering where the leisurely pace that so recently marked the Columbia Country had gone.

And everywhere there were changes.

Although the annual salmon spawning runs were still a major event, the Columbia River—while continuing to furnish food and power—was no longer the main life-line. Fur companies continued to compete for beaver and otter. But the transcontinental railroads now bound the Northwest to the East and northern heartlands, stimulating immigration and making wagon trains a thing of the past. Territories were becoming states ("unnatural," Doc George complained, like amputating a limb unnecessarily). Now, although the iron horse was siphoning the valley's produce from farm, forest, and pasture, it admittedly was a boon for the Kennedy Silver Mines—transporting freight and mail at reduced rates and giving faster service.

All this was "man's talk" to Courtney. But Cousin Bella lent a practiced ear. And Courtney herself paid more attention when Efraim made an infrequent visit in early April—fortunately on one of those rare evenings when Clint, Doc George, and Brother Jim were all present at the dinner table.

"The ocean-to-ocean railroad line is snaking toward Vancouver," Efraim told the group, "and Seattle's out-growing Tacoma. Port cities are making a bid, along with British Columbia, for trade with the Orient . . ."

That accounted for the pretty China-made toys in the shops, Courtney thought mistily—the toys she had hoped to have a need for before now. The time would come.

She forced herself to listen, feeling that somehow the conversation would be revealing. It was.

"I hear," Clint commented, "that Washington's population is rising rapidly."

Efraim nodded. "Some 375 percent—a sudden onslaught. The railroads are getting government grants which allow 400-foot-wide right-of-ways and a checkerboard of 640-acre sections per mile—pardon me, ladies, I do not wish to be a bore, but I do have a point to make. Land is going at a premium now—"

"What are you suggesting, Efraim?" Cousin Bella demanded in her come-to-the-point voice.

"Simply that my partner is eager to close the deal for Rambling Gate—and, while I have backed away—"

Doc George cleared his throat. "Tell Mr. VanKoten that Arabella Kennedy has decided against the investment!"

Efraim looked relieved. And Courtney let out a silent sigh of relief. This, she decided was not the time to make mention of strange sightings—hers or Donolar's.

She saw that Donolar's mind was whirling in reckless disorder. It was a relief when he began a death passage from Shakespeare, only to resort to mumbling something about his butterflies. Maybe even they warred among themselves . . . and which side should he take in case of battle?

Courtney wanted to share Lance's letter with Efraim, but he lingered downstairs after coffee. Besides, the letter had little to do with his plans. It was she and Clint who would go when weather permitted. Meanwhile, her brother's mind was heavily occupied. She wrote a note to Roberta, inviting her to spend the following week as a guest at the Mansion-in-the-Wild.

"Will you deliver this to Miss VanKoten?"

"My privilege," Efraim said absently. He was listening intently to Brother Jim who was expressing a need for a larger building if the congregation kept expanding.

"I've been looking a little harder and deeper into each man I meet—friend and foe alike—of late," he confessed. "Seems to me that as I study the gospel stories, I've been getting a new insight. You know, Jesus walked with the common man—looked deep into his heart for the good that was there, no matter how mean and ornery. The gun-slingin' moonshiners, the crazy-drunks, and even the prostitutes! Shocking, but true. I've been searchin' the Scripture. Jesus loves 'em all!"

Yes. And Courtney must do some searching, too. Her own heart first. Then trying to find what lay below the surface of Mother . . . Roberta . . . and Horace Bellevue, her distant cousin and now her brother-in-law. It was the New Law Jesus brought.

CHAPTER 23
The New Woman

All the week following, Courtney and Roberta worked together on what they called the New Woman. Roberta, in spite of her original shyness and her keen mind for business, was surprisingly good company. All business one minute and extremely vulnerable the next. And, on occasion, a sense of humor—like a hidden spring—bubbled up to surprise them both. Courtney found the girl appealingly eager to please. And by Friday, when Roberta was scheduled to return to the city, the two were close friends.

One thing, however, puzzled Courtney. It was obvious that Roberta was frightened. Fear revealed itself in the trembling of the long, lean hands and the way she had of biting her underlip—not to mention a haunted look in the oversized eyes.

"Something is troubling you, Roberta," Courtney had ventured the first day. "Do you feel we can talk about it?"

Roberta drew a sharp breath as if here, too, were an enemy. "The inner woman shapes the outer," Courtney encouraged.

"I—I am afraid of failing again," Roberta said softly.

"Again?"

Roberta nodded. "I am a disappointment to Father— my gender, my appearance—"

Courtney laughed lightly. "The gender we can do nothing about. But we *can* make you proud to be a woman. I promise!"

"There's more," Roberta said shyly. "I—I would like to have your brother—well, see me—"

Courtney gulped. Maybe she had promised too much. No, she hadn't! "Once you have stated your problem, you are well on your way to handling it!" she said with assurance.

"You are so courageous, Courtney."

Courageous? Time would tell. She longed to go into detail about her own turbulent life, her insecurities, and—yes—the fears that lay ahead. Instead, she smiled at Roberta.

"So you want to be beautiful? Well, a wise but strict lady told me in finishing school that first we have to learn to walk! Head held high—higher!"

"But—that makes me too tall!" Roberta protested, her pale face coloring with embarrassment.

"In height there is dignity. Stand tall, Roberta—that's it! Now, walk back and forth—chin up! Think of yourself as a queen—no, better yet, remember with pride that we are pioneer women here on the frontier, no matter what our backgrounds. The world will always be in need of pioneers, even after our men have conquered this land of forests and rivers and the savages that so-called civilization brings. There will always be new jungles to clear— prejudice, malice, poverty, ignorance."

"Discouraging, isn't it?"

Roberta, still pacing back and forth the width of the bedroom floor, head still high, paused. "May I stop now?"

Courtney examined the other girl's profile. The deep- set eyes. The bold eyebrows. But, most of all, a sort of gentleness she saw in the face. No hardness. That gave her courage to go on.

"Of course, it is time to stop—and get on to other things. And, no, I am *not* discouraged—no matter which subject you addressed the question to. I am neither dis- couraged about our project nor am I discouraged about the pioneer spirit. In a sense, Roberta, they are one and the same."

"Good! In spite of the impression I give, I come from fighting stock!"

"Then how can we fail? We will carry on with a kind of continuity. Growing, always growing." Courtney paused. What she was about to undertake was like dipping her toe into ice water. "God needs pioneers, too—"

Roberta sighed. "How different our lives have been."

The timing seemed right. "Not so different, my dear Roberta—come closer. We are going to be open with one another, so let me tell you that, while your dress is lovely, the dressmaker did not fit it to your figure—"

Again the sigh. "My fault. I insisted on looseness. I am so *bony*. As comfortable as I feel with you, Courtney, I feel like a St. Bernard looking down at a poodle! Oh," (clapping her hand over her mouth) "what have I said!"

Courtney laughed lightly. "Expressed yourself—and I like that. Cara Laughten has a sewing machine and I *want* those beautiful bones to show. You'll look like a model from *The Godey Book*! But the color—hmmm, brown does nothing for you really. Let's try a yellow scarf. Now!" she said triumphantly. "See how the color brings out amber spokes in your eyes?"

Roberta gasped in surprise, lingering at the mirror.

"Don't be vain," Courtney teased. Roberta turned away reluctantly and as Courtney nipped the dress in at the waist and straightened the hem as she had seen Cara do, she told the other girl of her own loneliness, her insecurities, and the love she had found here. Clint. Family. And a Greater Love.

"My father knows the Bible from cover to cover—you know *his* mind—but it was an intellectual pursuit. I need more."

"That's a start," Courtney said, taking pins from her mouth. She meant the statement both ways—Roberta's make-over and God's love. Something warned CAUTION.

The next day they worked on Roberta's hair—rainwater rinse . . . plain pompadour . . . and ringlets (thanks to Cousin Bella's curling iron) about the high forehead and at the nape of the neck.

When Clint came home on Wednesday night, his eyes widened in admiration. "A new guest!" he said. "A new woman!"

Both ways, Courtney's heart whispered.

"He meant it—he really did!" Roberta said in awe moments later. And then, "We'll try me out on the ghosts tomorrow!"

CHAPTER 24
Ghosts?

Courtney felt a sense of foreboding as she and Roberta set off for Rambling Gate. One she was unable to explain—especially when the sky was pure turquoise. The trees, so recently stripped and bare between a skeleton hedge, were now capped with crowns of new leaves. The evergreen ferns waved a welcome in air so pure it forced sojourners to breathe deeply. Courtney drew a long, ecstatic breath which came out in a sigh of uncertainty. Roberta took no notice.

"Such a shimmering day—like the Day of Creation," Roberta breathed. The words sounded more like her own than her friend's, Courtney thought. And, at her look of surprise, Roberta stammered self-consciously, "I—well, that's what Efraim calls such a morning—I—"

"I am glad the two of you have such conversations."

"Don't let me exaggerate—I—we have had a few, but—" squaring her shoulders in the newfound way, she said lightly, "maybe there will be more. First, let's see how the ghosts receive us."

Courtney was about to say that such talks as Roberta and Efraim shared, though brief, formed a firm foundation. That Clint's Dream-Country talk tied heaven and earth together for her—the ladder upon which she had climbed to take God's hand.

What stopped her? Perhaps the mention of ghosts. "You don't really believe those stories, Roberta? About Rambling Gate's being haunted?"

"I think something is going on there. And before my father takes on the restoration—your cousin consenting—"

Roberta's voice trailed off. "Did you hear something?"

"Just the wind whining in the trees."

"No, something else. Like the hoot of an owl—only it's the wrong time of day. Besides, I think they are hooted out after last night!"

"It would be rare if the creatures—I do not like them either!—hooted in the daylight hours. It could have been the crows."

Courtney's voice sounded uncertain even to her own ears. There *were* crows overhead. But, in her imaginative state, they became witches of the night, creeping from some black dream.

"There it is!" Courtney said in relief as they came out of the dense woods and she caught sight of the old mill. "Be careful crossing that rickety bridge—if you still want to go?"

"I do!" Roberta said. "I have borrowed from your courage—"

Further conversation was impossible. The roar and splash where the stream widened to meet with the river drowned out the spooky noises of the forest behind them. But ahead?

Rambling Gate looked even less inviting than before. Courtney longed to touch Roberta's sleeve. But Roberta had called her courageous. And she was knocking—

Knocking? Did she really think that the place was inhabited? Courtney shivered. How foolish! Ghosts needed neither fires nor lights . . . even if they existed.

Noiselessly, Roberta turned the rusty knob. With a squeak of protest, the door yielded.

"No ghosts—unless they're out on some expedition—"

The sentence hung in midair as there came a faint squeak like that of an ungreased buggy wheel. Courtney imagined that she heard Roberta's heart over the wild beat of her own. But before either was able to speak, there was a raspy call. "Who's thar?"

Courtney's heart was hammering so hard that she had failed to hear the creaking wheels grow louder, then stop. The room was in total darkness, but there was the musty scent of aging flesh, rotting wood, and stale food.

Again the raspy voice. "That you, Miz Villard? I kep' waitin' like ye said—jest a-waitin' 'n waitin'—or did one o'them nice men brang me peppermints?"

Villard? That was generations ago. But *nice men?*

Roberta recovered before Courtney. At least, she regained her voice to say they were not Mrs. Villard. They were—

Courtney concentrated on the crone-like creature wearing a yellowed frill of a cap that identified her as a maid. A maid, straining toward the century-mark in a wheelchair near the same age.

"Speak yore piece. I ain't seein' so good. Who be it?"

A gnarled hand held an ancient trumpet to her ear.

"We didn't intend frightening you—" Roberta began.

"T'weren't ye what skeered me," the old woman mumbled.

But somebody. Courtney's eyes had adjusted only enough to see that the frightened eyes, like matching jet beads set in a shrunken face as wrinkled as a black walnut, strained to see her guests. All to no avail. She frowned, rearranging the wrinkles, then huddled farther into the welter of ragged shawls.

"Best ye be a-goin' 'fore Miz Villard be a-comin. She's a-gonna be brangin' me peppermints an' th' greedy 'uns might be a-takin' 'em—whad'd ye say yore names be?"

Again the great horn to the sagging ear. Again the look of fear. "Roberta VanKoten, Ma'm, and my friend—"

"Stop a-screamin'. I ain't deaf! Now, be gittin'!"

Then the door slammed, as if blown by an unseen wind. Only there was no wind, no breeze at all. Someone else was present!

Both girls hurried through the maze of thistles and blackberry vines, neither bothering to follow the ancient stepping-stone path—once elegant and now countersunk in dead grass.

"What do you make of it?" Roberta's bravado was gone.

"I—think that there was someone else in the house— there, Roberta, I *did* hear the owl. The poor soul, who- ever she is, had good cause for warning us—"

"Listen!" Roberta's whisper interrupted Courtney. "An answering hoot. *Courtney*, the sounds are not from owls. They—are human signals—warnings! Give me your hand—let's run!"

CHAPTER 25
Potpourri

Donolar's "going away" gift was much like the talk that ensued. Potpourri. Miss VanKoten's visit was finished.

Roberta, breathlessly awaiting the arrival of her father (and hopefully, she confided to Courtney, Efraim would accompany him), went into the dining room early to watch Donolar arrange the first of his yellow rosebuds. Courtney, having taken great pains with Roberta's toilette, hurried through her own. She had forgotten to suggest to Roberta that no mention be made of the strange presence at Rambling Gate—especially not to her impressionable brother.

And so it was that she, too, entered the room well before the appointed dinner hour. At the door, Courtney paused to admire her handiwork. Cara had willingly fitted the dresses Roberta had brought. Roberta, pleased with the results, planned to have a dressmaker alter the ones left in the city. Tonight she was wearing a soft yellow-striped gown which shaded to a near-orange in the glow of the firelight. The hair, so recently drab, picked up the bronze tones and teased the pompadour and soft curls into dancing with gold. Donolar, too, was impressed.

"By cultivating the beautiful we scatter the seeds of heavenly flowers . . ." He blushed and turned aside without finishing the quotation. "I have a gift for you— potpourri from my garden, sachet made from my roses, with the help of spices borrowed from Mandy's kitchen."

Shyly, he handed a small jar of sun-dried rose petals to Roberta. "Oh, Donolar," she said with appreciation. She opened the container and immediately the air was scented with a blend of cinnamon, grated nutmeg, vanilla beans, roses, and pine gum from the crackling fire.

Taking note of her pleasure, Donolar began a detailed account of his recipe. It took a lot of "rose hunting." Roses must be captured while dew-damp . . . spread out to dry for weeks . . . then some premium petals pressed for decoration . . .

"But never venture out at night because of the evil ones that lurk in the dark. And sometimes they come in the mornings—unless the butterflies are around to protect you. I saw your tracks this morning and followed. I tried to signal—"

His words were the gapseed that caused Roberta's mouth to fly open. Just as quickly, she closed it and sighed in obvious relief. "Then the hoots were our warning?"

"Oh, no! Owls are evil creatures. The call of a valley quail is my secret warning to Courtney—"

"Donolar, let's not alarm our guest. I—we—"

But Courtney was unable to go on. She had caught sight of Clint's eyes burning into hers in the mirror above the buffet. The perfect cameo of his face against the dark wood paneling. The set of the chin. And the hard line of his usually generous mouth. Clint looked for a moment like a displeased schoolmaster. Was he dismissing her? She wondered how much he had heard.

Too much, she was to learn just minutes later. Even as she murmured "Clint!" and rushed into his arms like a guilty child, the clock was striking. There were voices on the stairs. The family entered—Cousin Bella, Doc George, Brother Jim, Mandy, and Mrs. Rueben (side-by-side, not in alliance, but lest one be elevated above the other in order of importance). Robert VanKoten. And *Efraim*!

Roberta obediently lifted her cheek for her father's kiss. But her eyes sought Efraim's, met them, and read the admiration she had so hoped to see.

But it was Robert VanKoten who spoke. "I say now, *is* this my daughter? My dear, you look smashing—absolutely smashing."

Roberta laughed with newfound confidence. "Thank you, Father. And, since you have reverted to your English adjectives, may I say that I am jolly well pleased?"

There followed the seating, prayers, and then small talk. Then, uncharacteristically, Donolar muttered, "I wish that my sister and her fair guest were more like Juliet."

Efraim laughed. "Juliet, Donolar? Are they not more fair?"

"They lack her insight of tragedy. Her sense of timing. 'I have no joy in this contract tonight; it is too rash, too ill-advised, too sudden.' "

"Meaning?" Clint's voice held a steel edge. "What do you know of Rambling—or shall I say *Gambling* Gate, Donolar?"

Roberta came to the defense of Donolar and Courtney.

"Donolar fears the place and probably with just cause. As for Courtney, she had nothing to do with our going."

"Neither of them is on trial, Miss VanKoten!" Cousin Bella's voice was as finely honed as her nephew's.

Such a few days ago Roberta would have felt backed into a corner. But the New Woman lifted her chin without showing signs of feeling threatened.

"I apologize if I gave the impression that I believed Courtney was unable to speak for herself. But I do think it is time we bring all the facts into the open, get to the bottom, see who—if anybody—has prior claim."

"Spoken like a true attorney-at-law," Robert VanKoten's voice carried a ring of pride.

Roberta thanked him with her eyes. Probably the first compliment he had given her, Courtney thought—no, the second! He had spoken with approval upon seeing her hidden beauty unveiled.

Spurred to converse in a new way with her father, Roberta said simply, "My motivation was to investigate the property in question, get a feel for its reconstruction, and possibly glean something of its mysteries of the past—and present."

Her father leaned forward. "And did you?"

Roberta told of the eerie silence surrounding Rambling Gate . . . the peculiar timing of hooting owls—more like human imitations—and the wrinkled crone who greeted them.

At that point, everybody began talking at once. Who could the woman be? What was she doing there? Any hint as to her identity?

"No," Roberta admitted, "but she had been a maid judging by the leftover scrap of lace, part of a uniform. She made little sense, saying she was waiting for Mrs. Villard. Which, of course, is impossible—so long ago—"

"Not at all," Brother Jim boomed. "Could mean Alexis, the harlot! She was a Worthington, married once to a Villard."

"But the strange lady made mention of *nice men*, then in contradiction, the *greedy ones*. No, Brother Jim, sir, it could hardly be Alexis Villard. Her name, according to our records is now Bellevue—"

"The Brothers!" Donolar shrieked, upsetting his soup.

"It's all right, Donolar," Cousin Bella soothed. "I put nothing past that woman. She is like a chameleon who puts on 'heirs' and changes hues—as well as names—when it serves her purpose. Now undoubtedly it serves her well to revert back to the Worthington-Villard alliance. That Milton Bellevue would stop at nothing to gain an end. And no longer being incarcerated—"

"Clint," Doc George broke in to observe, "why so silent? I have seen neither hair nor hide of Horace lately. Do you still trust him?"

Clint frowned. "He's pushing for a promotion, nothing more. Still, I suggest caution—more than my Courtney showed today."

He reached beneath the tablecloth to squeeze her hand. "I will make you a prisoner in our own house unless you promise—"

"To love and obey," Doc George said. "Remember your health!"

CHAPTER 26
Even from Afar

Toward the end of April, rain came to bless the farmers' crops. The few days when Courtney was unable to take her daily walks, she caught up on writing in her journal. Clint often took it with him to the mines, giving her no opportunity to write daily. But her notes were copious.

There was a gracious note of appreciation from Roberta to Courtney. How could she ever repay her, Roberta wondered. Her entire life had taken a new turn in ways that were too private to explain. Courtney smiled. *There is no need for explanations.*

And Roberta won Cousin Bella's heart completely with her proper "bread and butter" letter. Never had it been her privilege to be received by such a charming hostess— not exactly as a guest, more like a member of a wonderful family.

"Which the young lady well may become, Courtney," Cousin Bella said. "She will one day be a gracious hostess herself. It would please me to see her as the mistress of Rambling Gate—"

She stopped as if suddenly aware of having honored the estate with a name. "You know," Cousin Bella dreamed aloud, "since I decided against competing for the property—hoping to present it to you and Clint—I could accomplish it another way. That is, seeing it in the hands of a Glamora."

"Why, Cousin Bella!" Courtney feigned surprise. "You are a born matchmaker."

"I did right well for you and Clint!" Arabella Kennedy said tartly. "And I suspect the gene of matchmaking runs in your veins as well. You have been giving off sparks since you married my nephew, wanting everybody to be as happy!"

Courtney's eyes grew misty. "Yes, and it was you who led me to understand that Jesus taught us to love our mates as He loves His Church. Such a beautiful comparison. You, too, who made me bold as I, in turn, passed the message to Roberta."

Cousin Bella's brows knitted into a frown. "Bold?"

Courtney laughed. "Bold enough to remind you that you have a gentle, kind, fun-loving man at your feet—just waiting for a mud puddle so he can spread his red velvet coat—"

Cousin Bella snorted. "More likely to push me in so he could administer a fatal dose of modern medicine—or homeopathic mare's milk and licorice root!"

"Probably," Courtney said, suppressing a smile, "in order to have a chance to treat you. Well," faking a sigh, "it is unfortunate that you can dish out advice so beautifully and not—"

"—take it myself? Who says I haven't asked myself a million times why I let go so easily? Asking also if I am able to start all over—letting the bitterness gradually dilute—picking up a mature relationship instead of growing into it?"

"Let *me* answer. Yes—yes, you are able. Providing you follow your own advice—letting nothing come between you two."

"And no*body*, my dear. Do you understand?"

Courtney understood. "My mother?" Her whisper hung between them.

"The same. She'll rule you from afar—if you allow."

*   *   *

Arabella Kennedy's prediction was destined to prove correct. It began with Lance's letter which arrived in the next mail delivery.

> My dearest Courtney:
> I fear for the Lady Ana's sanity. Your mother seldom arouses. It should be a source of comfort, I suppose, that your dear mother has accepted what she terms her "fate" . . . doomed to live out the brief remainder of her life . . . alone . . . unloved (so unlike her and so untrue . . . and alas, so unfair), her incoherent mumblings about reaching out from her grave to forgive you . . .

Forgive me? The emotional letter unearthed the old hurts, the old feelings of guilt. Neither Lance's expression of appreciation that Robert VanKoten had purchased his paintings and ordered more nor his half-promise to revisit lifted Courtney's dark veil of depression.

To make matters more difficult, Courtney was feeling unexplainably weary. Mirrors reflected an unnatural paleness of skin and deep circles beneath her eyes. Doc George took note and prescribed a tonic. Clint noticed, too, and—holding her tenderly in his arms—made her promise to sleep late the next morning. Four o'clock was too early for her to arise simply to see her husband off. Courtney would sit up all night, if necessary, but was too tired to say so. And so she promised.

The next morning she was glad. The scent of Mandy's powerful coffee, usually so inviting, set her stomach to churning. By noon, thankfully she felt fine—even welcomed the smell of wood smoke seasoned with the aroma of Mandy's pheasant stew, made rich and racy with onions and freshly ground pepper.

"Feeling better, sweetheart?" Clint inquired that evening.

"Oh, much!" Courtney tiptoed to accept his kiss.

But the next morning, the nausea was back. And the next. When the queasiness became a pattern, Courtney knew. Not scientifically. But with a woman's instinct.

Later she was to wonder why she did not share her secret with Clint. Even then, she supposed, she had entertained the idea that Mother's welfare came before her own.

* * *

Efraim checked the weather conditions over the Pass by telegraphy. Trains were back on schedule. Would Courtney prefer that he made the trip East? Purchase of Rambling Gate hung in balance, but—

Oh, no, she and Clint needed a second honeymoon.

The rains had stopped. The Washington countryside was a riot of blossoms. The nausea had passed. Why then the lethargy? Could she have been wrong? Courtney dared not consult with Doc George. She was driven, as if by some demon, to respond to her mother's cry of helplessness . . .

CHAPTER 27
Discovery

Courtney learned to pace herself. Sleep later in the mornings followed by a walk. A nap in the afternoon. And then another walk.

It was at the close of the later walk that Courtney found Clint at home long before he was due. Preparations for an early-morning shipment of silver were made and he had sent the men home early, he explained. But why was he smiling so secretively about it? He wore the happiest face she had ever seen on a man!

"You look like Mouser, the cat, after lapping a saucerful of cream! Do you know something I don't?"

"No! But I now know something you *do* know! Oh, Courtney, I'm happy (he kissed her), *happy* (he kissed her again), HAPPY!"

By the third kiss, Courtney had decided the source of his joy made no difference. She felt the same happiness—as if his blood were transfused into her own veins.

The thought brought an immediate suspicion. "How—how did you discover my secret—so prematurely? I told only God."

Already the proud father, Clint laughed deeply and richly. "Don't you think men have instincts?"

"You *knew*?"

"After cramming for this exam. You see, I decided to catch up on my reading." Clint pulled the journal—now up-to-date—from behind him. He sobered and became not only the proud, but the anxious father. "We must see Doc George at once—"

"I am fine, darling—just fine. Remember I have been in training for ever so long. And I have a special book that cautions against building up hopes too early. I will take care—if you will stop squeezing me—no, *don't* stop! Not ever!"

"I won't, my precious madonna." His voice held the reverence of a prayer.

* * *

The announcement should be made to all the family at one sitting, Courtney and Clint decided. That way nobody would feel favored over the other. They timed the announcement to coincide with a time when Efraim would be home.

There were whoops of joy when Clint said in a carefully planned understatement, "Mr. and Mrs. Clinton Desmond are going to become parents." Courtney heard only the din of voices, as her heart swelled in her breast. Excitement reached a feverish pitch, each member offering advice—even suggesting names for the latest heir.

Yes, yes, she would take care. What choice had she with such a hovering father-to-be? A Christmas baby? Courtney was unsure but (with a warning look at Doc George) she *was* sure of the conception. Yes, Donolar, a real, live baby. Yes, Cousin Bella, they would need a suite now. And yes, Mandy and Mrs. Rueben, she would need them both. More than ever!

"Brother Jim, we will be needing *you* all the way through," Courtney said bravely. "You see, Clint and I will break with tradition. We plan to follow Doc George's book about prenatal influences. I refuse to go into confinement, so will give this child the best influence of all—gifting the young Desmond with an early start by bringing the baby to church *in utero*!"

"Unborn!" Donolar said wisely.

"Praise de Lawd!" Mandy near-shouted. The others said, "Amen!"

Efraim stayed overnight. He and Clint talked at length. It was unsafe for Courtney to travel. Efraim said with a hint of pride that he would go, of course. Roberta could take over. She was as wise as she was beautiful.

Evenings were longer now. Saturday was Clint and Courtney's first chance to be alone. Why not take a sunset walk so they could talk? But they were as strangely quiet as they had been on their honeymoon. The moment was too sacred to defile with words. They watched, in sacred silence, the sunset's rosy afterglow fade to rich amber . . . listened to the lullaby of the wind in the pines . . . and, forgetting the dinner hour (and knowing they would be forgiven), watched the sky burst into starry splendor. Venus, the undisputed lovers' star, looked down with approval.

And, briefly, Mother and Rambling Gate were forgotten.

CHAPTER 28
Warnings

Courtney's thoughts rushed ahead! June . . . July . . .
August . . . September with a burst of crimson-and-
gold foliage . . . November with warm fires, wild turkey, and all the other things that spelled out Thanksgiving. Courtney wished she knew when the baby would
choose to arrive. Christmas with its blessed message of
love . . . the tallest tree imaginable adorned with the
hand-carved toys she and Clint had seen on their honeymoon. Rag dolls? A bobsled? *Both?*

Anticipation of the glory of each season consumed
her. As if seeking a sign, Courtney had Donolar saddle
Peaches. "You must learn to let Baby and me ride double,"
she whispered to the little mare. "I had planned that we
would decide on the season that was best—but, for now,
let's put it to rest. You and I will rest, too. I feel unbeliev-
ably tired." How could this be? She was carrying the
beginnings of a very small baby—

Courtney was almost dozing when the welcome sight
of Mansion-in-the-Wild came back into view. And she
stumbled as she entered the front door quietly—trying to
remember how many steps she must climb before reaching the upper story. One . . . two . . . three , . .

Courtney staggered just as she reached the landing
that divided the two stories. Only to be caught by two
loving arms. Clint! She had failed to see his horse. And
what was he doing home at noon?

Clint held her closer, concern in his lake-blue eyes.
Courtney was too exhausted to speak. But even in her

faraway world she relished the strength of the muscles beneath his rough wool shirt. Gently, he laid her on their bed and spread a lightweight quilt over her.

"Stay put, my darling," he comforted, tucking the quilt beneath her feet. "I'm going for Mandy. Cousin Bella has taken your place with Brother Jim—if you can imagine. Mandy will watch over you until I get Doc George—I saw his buggy—"

Clint's voice seemed to recede. When Mandy brought soup and hot sassafras tea with toasted muffins, Courtney could only shake her head. There was deep gratitude inside her, but exhaustion robbed her of speech.

Courtney was only faintly aware of Doc George's voice. "This young lady takes chances, Clint. She may or may not be pregnant—early to tell yet—but I'm guessing she could be, in view of her fatigue. But that could be a warning signal! Make it clear that she is not, repeat, is *not* to ride horseback! Our Courtney has been under far too much stress . . . give her two of these along with a swat from the hairbrush . . . and get her in bed!"

"I *am* in bed!" Courtney wanted to point out. But Doc George was taking his leave and Clint was unbuttoning her shoes. Slipping off her blouse. And clumsily trying to ungird her body from the manacles of her undergarments.

"Lift your head, my darling—there, just a bit—"

Courtney felt the welcome brush of flannel as her head popped through the neck of the nightie.

"I will sit with you until you sleep . . ."

But she *was* asleep.

Hours later Cousin Bella's voice entered her dark world, advancing and receding with Clint's voice in between. Careful not to disturb her, there were no lights in the shadowy room.

"Somehow we must force her to take care . . . best not to worry her with George Washington's warnings . . . 'twould destroy the darling if something went wrong . . ."

"Nothing's going wrong!" Clint's words had the ring of being spoken through clenched teeth. "Nothing!"

"I will watch over her, make her my prisoner since you are unable to be here—especially with all the shipments going out and Efraim gone. By the way, Clint, why *are* you home at noon?"

Clint's voice dropped even lower. "Somebody is scaring Donolar out of his wits . . . hooting and screeching. Somehow I feel that this is no figment of his imagination. But we must keep our concerns quiet as I check the matter out, Aunt Bella. My heart tells me so—and yet my instincts warn that Courtney should know in case of real danger—"

Crash! And then the musical tinkle of broken glass.

"What in the world? A rock—thrown through our window?"

Silence. Clint's footsteps. And then his answer to Cousin Bella. "A note—a warning. It says: 'CAUTION: STAY AWAY FROM GAMBLING GATE!' "

CHAPTER 29
The Horrible Truth

Had she only dreamed it? The fatigue had passed. Viewed in retrospect, maybe it was less draining than Courtney remembered. Maybe there had been no warnings about her health, about—well, what was it about anyway? Was anything ever as horrible or as wonderful as it seemed afterwards?

Yes—yes, it was, she answered her own question. Love was as wonderful! Her love for Clint grew with each day they spent together. Courtney clung to him. Refusing to let him out of her sight. Made him *her* prisoner instead of the other way around. And ignored the little voice that cried for a response to the niggling question as to why he was here. Until the fatal morning.

Just last night the two of them had walked in the orchard-scented twilight, watched the stars bediamond the purple enameled sky, as the moon—in its second phase—discreetly regarded the lovers' kisses with its eye half-closed. This morning, although it was not yet light, Courtney reached for Clint's hand. They always began their walk early and were home for Mandy's hearty breakfast with ravenous appetites.

But there was no hand to respond. No Clint. And his side of the bed was cold!

Alarmed, Courtney rose and, without lighting a lamp, tiptoed down the long hall to look out the window of the tower. Somehow she had known there would be a light in Donolar's cabin. Just as she had known that he would not be there when, minutes later, she knocked on his door. It all came back then. The warnings had been no dream. There *was* danger. Undoubtedly, the sounds had been repeated. Donolar had alerted Clint and he had gone to check on Rambling Gate! It was unlikely that Clint would have allowed her brother to tag along. Why, then, was Donolar missing? He must have left hurriedly—too hurriedly to snuff out the candle. That in itself could be dangerous—cause a fire—

Her heart beating a tattoo, Courtney picked up the candle snuffer. A noise! It could have been the scuttling of a mouse behind the chair rail or an antelope crashing through the outside underbrush. The drumming of her pulse made it impossible to differentiate. Instinctively, she dropped the snuffer, drew in a trembling breath, and blew hard. The room was darkened except for a crack in the burlap drapes. Through it Courtney saw the morning star wink out to make way for the pale pink arrival of early dawn. But something was wrong—something having to do with the giant tree beside the cabin. The trunk was too thick. And then a shadow disengaged itself from the tree trunk and, head bent low, eased into the forest. The outline was unmistakably that of a man. Even in that hunchbacked position, the figure was vaguely familiar.

Trying to still her heart, Courtney stood motionless. She had left the door unlatched and through it there came the welcome, sweet two-note call of a quail. Donolar!

Courtney's first impulse was to call his name in relief. But something warned her. And when the call was repeated she knew what was wrong. Donolar's signal had come from the opposite direction of the disappearing figure. Fearing for him, yet hardly daring exhale, she searched for him in the heavy shrubbery over her left shoulder, hoping that he had sought refuge in the Mansion gardens. At the same time, she glanced to the right toward Rambling Gate. The sun, as if hesitating to rise from behind the mountains, sent up a warning flare— jagged spikes as pale as Donolar's pink roses. A rosy glow spread slowly to the treetops. She *must* find Donolar. Both of them must be clearly visible—if they hadn't been spotted already—

It was Donolar who made the first move. He was by her side. Holding her hand. Trying to say "they" had been there. Well, anyway, *one*. Maybe more. They must warn Clint—

And then they both heard a faint sound. A stone, undoubtedly disturbed by a human foot, had left its resting place on the trail and was bouncing with gathering momentum in its rush to the ravine below. Then, much farther away, there was a low, cautious "Who— hoo!" Immediately, farther away yet, came an answering hoot. Human signals as to each other's whereabouts? Or the message that she and Donolar had turned toward Rambling Gate?

Only love for Clint made Courtney stouthearted. It was silly to entertain the fear that an unseen presence was keeping pace with her and Donolar. Even when faintness threatened to overtake her, Courtney rushed ahead—deeper and deeper into the dark canopy of trees that made increasing daylight an underwater blue-green as the sun tried to penetrate the maze of overlapping trees corded by wild grape vines. Only when Donolar whimpered did she dare cast a furtive glance over her shoulder to put a silencing finger to her lips. Some inner voice urged her forward. But a cry from Donolar, giving away their whereabouts, stopped her in her tracks. From a distance came a murmurous drone of voices. Could her brother have sighted some hideous monster? A legion of them? A thrill of horror drew every nerve taut, refused to let her feet move.

Another cry from Donolar brought her to her senses.

Courtney whirled to see a trickle of crimson dripping from the thin skin of his slender hands. "The bushes try to stop us," he whispered. "They have claws—claws like the monsters—"

"There are no monsters, Donolar. Be very quiet." With an effort, she broke the hypnotic spell of the forest, took a handkerchief from her pocket, and wound it about his wounds. "Be brave. Concentrate on that patch of sky just ahead. Doesn't it resemble a turquoise—all streaked—"

"—with the matrix of clouds tinted with morning sun! But, oh, Courtney—I'm scared! I *can't* be brave!"

"That's why you *can* be brave, darling," Courtney urged in a guarded voice above the pounding of her own heart. "If you weren't scared, there would be no need for courage! That is why God gave us fear, the stepping-stone to courage."

A twig snapped below them, freeing her feet. "We must run, Donolar—run faster than we have ever run before—find Clint—"

Diverted by her words, Donolar nodded. "Yes, yes—like the Red Queen who told Alice 'Faster, faster'!"

Faster. *Faster* . . . but, even as they ran, a sense of futility seized her. Something was gaining on them, coming up from the ravine, cutting them off from the trail to Rambling Gate.

And there, blocking her way it was. No, not *it. He.* Horace Bellevue! "Don't try to escape. Courtney, be sensible. *Listen* to me!" He grasped her shoulders.

"Let my sister go," Donolar screamed. "Let go or I shall smash your head with a stone. I have *courage!*"

"Both of you do—which may be your undoing," Horace Bellevue panted. "I've been watching—trying to help—"

Courtney wrenched herself free. "You—you *lunatic!* That was you at Donolar's cabin!"

Her claws, resembling those of the blackberry vines, dug at the pale face swimming before her vision. "Don't touch me—ever again. You're a traitor. *You* threw that rock wrapped with a warning through the bedroom window. Run, Donolar, *run!*"

Wildly Courtney and Donolar ran. Even as from behind them came the words of Clint's half-crazed brother.

"If I am a traitor, it is only because of you! Yes, I was watching—guarding you both—under Clint's command! Wait—*please*—"

The next words were lost by the sound of breaking brush as Clint's half-brother hurled himself into the ravine, then vanished.

Courtney's body shook. Her throat was parched. But she raced on, with Donolar at her heels . . .

* * *

After it was all over, Courtney had difficulty putting the story in chronological order. She recalled having positioned Donolar behind a stump surrounded by head-high ferns, telling him to stay put. His ragged breathing told her that he would. Wind-bent bristlecone pines— older than Methuselah, and the only members of the species that ventured this far West, Robert VanKoten had pointed out—formed a witch-cave backdrop for the remains of Gambling Gate. The door of the ruins of the once-sprawling house (turned gambling hall) was standing open. From inside came the metallic sound of the lid of a kettle rising and falling to emit steam. But what was the strange *swish-swish* sound? The turn of a crank? But the mossy mill wheel was at rest.

Otherwise, all was silent. Until the hoot from the ravine. An answering "Who-hoo" from inside. And the hunched-over form of a man entering.

Courtney squatted low and hugged the trunk of an enormous fir, sickened by the smell of moth balls, rotting timber, and what was the other scent? Paint? No. Ink, maybe?

But she made no effort to identify sounds or scents. Her whirling mind was abuzz with the awful truth. Horace Bellevue *had* to be a part of this scam—whatever it was.

All was silent. And yet Courtney had an unreasonable sensation of a gathering audience. Above her a golden peephole broke through the density of the trees like a slit in a ragged curtain. Opening slowly. Allowing the actors backstage to squint at the spectators.

Donolar must have noticed. He uttered a cry that was a cross between a groan and a sob. ". . . all flesh is grass . . ."

There was no time to give a signal for silence. The tragedy had begun. The tragedy which would spawn more tragedies.

And there *was* an audience. "Who—" But the second syllable of the frightening hoot was never completed. A hand touched Courtney's shoulder. The hand of Horace Bellevue.

No, no! That was impossible. He was inside. But he was speaking words of caution, begging her to be still. Words she could not distinguish. *Who, then, had entered?*

There was the explosion of gunfire. Without any plan of action, Courtney loosed herself from the tree trunk and emerged from the shadows just as Alexis streaked from the door only to be grabbed from behind by Clint. Inside her, Courtney's heart exploded, too. Clint, her Clint, had entered Rambling Gate, passing as Horace. And he was hurt. Only Horace's arm restrained her as the tragic play unfolded.

Unable to make the getaway she had planned, Alexis changed tactics immediately. Tossing her head backward so that the sun stroked every wave of her flaming hair, she looked exactly as if waiting for a kiss. Even as the world exploded around them, Courtney had the near-unconquerable urge to hurl a rock into that beautiful face—hush that crooning voice that promised a reward. "Please let me go, Clint, my darling. None of the others meant anything to me—*please*, for old times' sake. You must care what happens—"

"I do indeed care. That's why we'll be holding you—"

Alexis's face was no longer beautiful. Her voice no longer caressing. "On what charge?"

At that point a man whom Courtney had never seen before stepped up behind Clint. "Officer of the law, Ma'm—and charges aplenty! You want numbers? I'll give you numbers. Number one, trespassing. Number two, harboring criminals. Number three, aiding and abetting. Number four, kidnapping that poor deranged woman—impersonating the *real* Mrs. Villard she used to work for. Number five, *possible* involvement in a federal crime. Agent Bellows, I have the lady cuffed. You take over from here—matter for our government!"

Courtney understood none of the charges. Her eyes were glued to the stream of blood coursing down her husband's arm. He was badly injured—perhaps fatally unless—

"Help, *help!*" She wrenched herself free from Horace.

"Courage, Courtney! You've managed to break all the rules. Get over there and rest until I can patch this man of yours together. What happened, Clint? Get yourself in a razor fight?"

Doc George! But how did he know to come? Courtney's mind and body gave way at the same time. Obediently, she sank onto a bed of ferns.

Courtney tried desperately to generate the energy to rise up . . . go to Clint . . . be sure of his safety. But it was as if she had no bones, no muscles, no central nervous system. Just a vague sense of viewing a stage performance from a seat that was too far away for the words and movements to make sense. But, of one thing she was sure. Clint was struggling to reach out to her, restrained less from weakness than from Doc George's bark of orders, "Get hold of him, Horace! You've served your brother well—continue!"

With the strength of Samson, Horace Bellevue pinned Clint to the ground. "Sniff this, Clint, while the doctor—"

Clint sniffed and coughed. Doc George stitched quickly and began wrapping bandages around the wounded arm. "The Lord was with you, son. The bullet barely missed an artery—"

And then Clint was bending over Courtney, his face—drained of all color—was filled with anxiety. "My darling, my brave, foolish little sweetheart—"

But Clint was being pulled away from her—when she needed him so much. But others needed him, too. *Who? Why*, she thought foolishly, *I am sounding like the hooters!*

More voices. And the next scene began. A parade. A parade led by Brother Jim! How did he—

But, listen to the words, Courtney willed herself.

"Take him, officer, before I am tempted to sin! I would take great pleasure in seeing this man toothless!"

"Now, now, Big Jimbo, show restraint! The Good Book cautions: 'Let your speech be always with grace,' " Doc George said.

"—'grace seasoned with *salt*,' " Brother Jim replied.

"Let me go, you dirty—" Courtney's ears did not hear the words. She was concentrating on a voice from the past. And even before she could force her eyes to focus on the face, she knew the voice belonged to one of the older Bellevues, followed by the other—and then Milton! Her vision clouded, but there was a blur of recently shaven heads, heavy stubble beards, and hawk eyes that saw everything at once. She had never thought they looked so alike—except for the eyes: the two older Bellevues' sharp and cunning; the two younger Bellevues' less cunning but too close to one another. And, of course, the two older half-brothers were always dirty while Milton had once been as nattily dressed as Horace. That was it—the *clothes*! Now all wore striped suits—the unmistakable prison uniform.

"Are you sure of identification? *Both* of you?"

"I should be," Horace was answering. "I have tailed them for Clint since they escaped. I thought they'd come here—with Milt's connection to that scarlet woman! But I never dreamed of the counterfeiting—"

Counterfeiting!

"And I rescued the woman Alexis kidnapped and made her believe herself the Mrs. Hillary who used to work here—and Alexis to be the mistress of Rambling Gate! Believe me, I had no part in the sordid affair."

"My brother is right," Clint said. "Now, if you will let me identify the evidence, gentlemen, I would like to check on the welfare of my wife. She is—well, if Mrs. Desmond will forgive my being so indelicate, I will add a ray of sunshine to this day of horrible truth. We are expecting our first child—"

It would have been a comedy, Courtney supposed, had the world not have been turned upside down. Men were offering congratulations, expressing concern, promising to get the records straight "forthwith"—while leading away a string of convicts and a lady with flaming hair to match her face.

The scene wavered. And, then, somehow they were making their way down the trail. Courtney hardly remembered the trip. Except that she had asked Clint, to whom she clung, how the mixture of law officers, criminals, the doctor, and the preacher happened upon the scene. Doc George overheard. "Why, intuition, my dear —intuition and the help of Arabella. Remember when she began riding with Big Jimbo—sort of a lady Paul Revere—"

Courtney heard no more. Clint was holding her closely and she clung to him. From love. And from need. The sky seemed to have fallen beneath her . . . the earth rising above.

*   *   *

The world had righted itself when at last Courtney spotted lavender smoke spiraling from the kitchen chimney of Mansion-in-the-Wild. That meant dear Mandy had started the evening meal. Donolar, half-singing, half-laughing that the hand of the Mighty had smitten the doers of evil, raced to his garden. Company. There must be fresh flowers.

It was then that Robert VanKoten, in stylish English tweeds, stepped out to meet the bedraggled group. Behind him, chin high, was Arabella Kennedy. Then Mandy and Mrs. Rueben. And all were asking questions at once. Courtney tried to concentrate, listen, respond. But a gray mist danced before her eyes, forcing her—once inside— to stop at the stair and grip the balustrade. The evening belonged to the family. She would measure up.

But she was unable. She clutched her throat to hold back the sob. Too late. Clint wheeled and rushed to her.

"Courtney, darling, it has been too much—oh, darling—"

Courtney heard through a silver fog. A fog that began to whirl. If only she could speak. The fog receded, then closed in. And then she crumpled.

Someone was massaging her wrists. Doc George was feeling for her pulse. And Cousin Bella was crying. She *never* cried. Mandy was praying. Brother Jim joined her prayers from afar.

The world steadied long enough for Courtney to look into Clint's pallid face. His eyes burned into hers. How tall he looked. His lips were so near—so near—but she was floating away like a boat broken loose from its mooring.

She fought for her life—no, not her life! The baby's . . .

CHAPTER 30
Posthumous World

Everyone was so kind. To no avail. Courtney was living in a posthumous world. She had died along with her baby. The smile she pasted on her face was artificial, because her heart was dead too. The words of family and friends were hollow placebos. Soothing syrup to satisfy the patient. But nobody could cut the umbilical cord. And nobody—*nobody*—could answer the crucial question: *Why?*

Dear Cousin Bella. How she had built dreams on the "heir to the throne." Courtney's old guilts crept in when she saw the tears in Arabella Kennedy's eyes as she said, "You are young yet, my dear. There will be another Kennedy."

Kennedy?

Yes, Kennedy Desmond. Kenny . . . later Ken . . . then . . .

Perhaps the baby would have been a girl. Courtney begged Doc George for an answer as to the lost child's gender.

"It was entirely too soon to tell, my child. You had little more than conceived—"

"But life had begun," Courtney said tonelessly.

The doctor stroked his beard thoughtfully. "Who am I to deny that? But, listen to me, Courtney. Not every acorn that hits the ground germinates. Not every pine nut becomes a tree even after it takes root."

"But there *was* germination—conception—"

151

"I wish I could read the Lord's mind, but I am only a country doctor. This I can say, miscarriages are not uncommon. Your mother, for instance, may have suffered several before knowing the joy of motherhood."

Something stirred within Courtney. "My mother would have welcomed her loss! Oh, why, *why*, WHY do babies often go to the wrong people?"

"Again, no answer. But, correct me if I'm wrong. Aren't you feeling a needless guilt as well as grief?"

Guilt? Yes. She had failed the Lord.

Brother Jim answered that one. "But not His purpose!"

She had failed Cousin Bella, Donolar . . . everybody . . . and especially Clint! How could Brother Jim understand?

Clint tried to wipe away her tears. Why did she hold back? Refuse to let him share her grief? He, too, had lost.

It was perhaps at the moment of her husband's attempted embrace that Courtney felt herself receding into the grave with the shadow of the beginnings of her firstborn. She would never do it again. It was too risky. Never take the chance of hurting like this . . . starting a life . . . only to destroy it.

CHAPTER 31
Going On

❦

Grief, translated into discouragement, is a ruthless killer. It can bring promising careers to a crippling halt. It can shatter flowering dreams. It can end marriages . . .

Oh, the possibilities were endless, Courtney knew. Somehow she must get on with the pretense of bearing up, for the sake of others. It was not right that those who brought food (tasteless as 'umble pie) must speak in hushed tones—several octaves below the distant sound of her baby's cry.

"An accident of nature," some said. Others shaking their heads in despair, declaring, " 'Tis th' Lord's will. "Sad 'bout th' miscarriage, but—"

Miscarriage. The word translated into "baby." And Courtney would clutch at her middle, wondering if it could be a mistake. But in her heart she knew. Doctors could help deliver babies. Doctors could help destroy them. Inside, Courtney wrapped herself in pain like a wounded animal curling up to protect itself. The pain belonged to her. If she lost it, she had lost the baby.

But she must think of Efraim's future . . . the Van-Kotens' dreams . . . the needs of the church and the settlement . . .

Clint? Somehow she put him last, even though his face was as pale as death, his eyes filled with pain and longing. She had failed him. And, in some unexplainable manner, he had failed *her*. There was a room in her heart that Courtney refused to let him enter.

Nevertheless, she began to function. She visited Cara, hoping to be able to let her feelings out. But sight of the fat cherubs, gold as apricots from the warm sunshine, only depressed her. She attended church, sitting stiffly beside Clint and responding without feeling to the warm greetings of the congregation afterwards. And she resumed the visitations with Doc George and Brother Jim.

"You're not fooling me, little one," Doc George said. "On the outside you're adjusting while on the inside you're brittle as pulled taffy. Let it out. Scream if you must, then get back into Clint's bed!"

Scream? If she started, she would never stop. And, as far as her husband was concerned, that was a private matter. Anyway, he was home so very little. He had neglected everything at the mines before the—the—no, she could not bring herself to say the horrible word. Now he was *neglecting* her.

Quickly, she pointed out a patchwork quilt of wild flowers. Only to regret it. The ground looked so *fertile!* Twining vines laced with flowers. Blackberries ready to make into jam. And everywhere the shouts of happy children.

CHAPTER 32
Shattering News

Gardens were at their July best the day Roberta dropped in unexpectedly. Stylish in a tweed riding skirt, she looked regal seated in the sidesaddle. Probably the first most in the settlement had ever seen, Courtney reflected as she embraced her friend.

"I'm genuinely glad to see you, Roberta!"

"I wanted to come earlier, Courtney—but I felt it inappropriate. I hope it is not too soon? You look so tired—"

"Come inside. Mandy will prepare us some coffee—or do you prefer tea?"

Small talk when her heart was breaking. She had lost her baby. Now she was losing her husband. She felt powerless. Out of control. There is no going back.

Somehow she managed to make conversation in an effort to gain control of herself. Rambling Gate was common ground.

Rambling Gate?

Oh, it was clear—belonged to the VanKotens. Efraim would be so pleased—

"I am sure he will be." Courtney paused and frowned. "I would have expected to hear from him by now."

"Oh, Courtney! *I* have! And there's so much to tell you! But, first let's walk to Rambling Gate. I've come to get ideas on decorating. Father has the original plans pieced together. They were tattered. But I was able to work them out like a puzzle and reconstruction will begin shortly. It's a heavenly day. No need for a shawl."

Courtney paused to look at her reflection. Pale. Wan. Hair drooping slightly from the forgotten 100 nightly strokes of the brush. And, for whatever reason, wearing the blue dress with the white collar and cuffs she had worn on arrival to the Washington Country. "I look rather dreadful," she murmured to the other Courtney in the mirror.

"Not dreadful, Courtney dear! But it grieves me to see you look so sad. You look like a little girl—lost—"

"Even the corners of my mouth are turned down. Most unbecoming." Courtney tried to speak lightly, but her voice broke.

"You have been hurt, that's why! And don't I know about hurting! But, Courtney, it was you who made me see life anew. Oh, that I could do the same for you. You see, from the moment my father brought me here I admired you tremendously. You were the nearest person I have laid eyes upon who qualified for the Storybook Princess—and you had your Prince Charming already. In trying to capture the attention of *my* Prince, I used you as my model—knowing how much he admired you. I copied your clothes, modified in style and color, and strove to master your graciousness. Don't let me down or I will never win him—"

"Efraim? But what do you mean about not letting you down, Roberta?"

"It was bold of me to speak my heart so openly about your brother when he has not declared himself. And I may have sounded critical of you—you, my dearest friend. But I need to see you as you were—so—so happy, with that forever look in your eyes—"

"Roberta—stop before you break my heart! You have in no way offended me. And there is nobody I would rather have marry my brother. It—it is just that I have failed again. Please don't add your name to the list of people I have failed—myself worst of all! Just never let

anything come between you and Efraim or your pur-
poses. Cling to him at any cost. Even when your heart
freezes over. You see, when it thaws, the hurt is still
there—eventually numbing you to the needs of others. I
am paying a terrible price for my double loss—"

"Courtney!" Roberta's face was ashen, her voice a
pained whisper. "You and Clint—are—not estranged?"

Courtney steadied herself by grasping Roberta's hand.
And immediately they were in each other's arms. Not
speaking. Just understanding. Each waging a private
war of thoughts—the spirit against the *self*. Which is
love's price.

"Thank you, Roberta. You *have* helped. Let me brush
my hair and change this dress!"

* * *

The woods seemed more friendly as the two girls
followed the needled trail. Courtney found it easy to talk
about the horrors she had endured there so recently.
Even the ruins of the ancient house looked less frightening.

"Being steeped in tradition as we VanKotens are, it is a
dream of my father's to restore the old place to its original grandeur down to the last detail," Roberta said excitedly as they walked down the stepping-stone walk. "A
mosaic table here," she went on as they reached the
overgrown garden, "right in the center of a warm,
fragrant court. We will have tea in the antique silver-
mounted porcelain cups Father had shipped from France.
And oh, Courtney, there will be a Gothic window on the
second floor offering a view of the court. Father even
wants nasturtium vines—the color of your dress, remember?"

Courtney nodded, a pain stabbing through her heart.

"Can't you just see a window box up there, trailing
vines bejeweled with yellow, gold, and bronze? And yes,

there should be topaz against the balcony. Can you see the background of walls in, say, pink—*pale* pink subdued by a shade of cream? Stone stairs, the plans said, and red velveteen drapes. I've ordered bolts and bolts— am I boring you?"

"*Boring* me? I see it with you, Roberta, just as I came to see this country through Clint's eyes—"

Roberta had the good sense not to pursue the subject. Instead, she said, "You will be pleased to know that Cara Laughten has agreed to make all the draperies. She is as clever as any of the designers—"

Courtney was caught up in the plans, feeling the first stirring of happiness. "How kind of you. Cara loves beautiful things. And believe me, she needs the money."

"So I gathered—with all that family—oh, there I've done it again. Forgive me, Courtney."

"Never mind apologizing, Roberta. It is impossible to avoid the subject forever. Tell me more about the house."

"Would you believe a sun pool? It's going to be like a Venetian palace—out of place here, I know, but we plan to put it to good use. *Make* it a part of the settlement, as your cousin has done. Rambling Gate—even when it was a den of iniquity—is a part of history, too."

Time passed quickly as Roberta explained that the pool would gather warmth from the sun. Children could wade in it. The mill wheel would remain, as would the ancient chests found inside. They would go inside and look, except that the hour was growing late. Yes, the cloud-patched sky had taken on the sleepy shade of afternoon.

Turning back to the Mansion, Courtney said, "All this will be beautiful, Roberta. I am happy for all of you. Now, tell me about Efraim's letter."

"Oh yes, Efraim knows that you will be unable to travel. He—he hasn't heard of your loss. So—well, Courtney—how can I break the news? He is bringing your mother here . . ."

CHAPTER 33
Farewell—Without a Kiss

Roberta left early the next morning. Courtney sought out Cousin Bella immediately. "We need to talk."

"Yes, we do." Arabella Kennedy, a study in black-and-white without adornment, looked all business. "Tell me about Miss VanKoten's plans for Rambling Gate."

Courtney quickly described how the rot and ruin of earlier days would be transformed to its original splendor.

Cousin Bella's head nodded up and down without disturbing the black hair woven with silver. "I remember! I will help Miss VanKoten if I am invited."

"Oh, Cousin Bella, you will be—providing—" she added teasingly, "you call Roberta by her name. She may be a bigger part of us than you realize."

Cousin Bella snorted. She detested having others think she was left out in the dark. Yet unsolved mysteries were "unconstitutional" in her code. Courtney wondered which would win out. When no question came, Courtney burst out without preamble, "Cousin Bella, there is something I must tell you—"

There she faltered and reached for her cousin's hand, feeling the need of something solid to cling to in life's tempestuous sea. She found it in the warming clasp of her kin. Brown eyes met brown eyes in mutual love and appreciation. Now it would be easier to talk.

"Roberta had a letter from Efraim. My mother is coming—they could arrive at any time. I—I don't know how to handle it—" Courtney's voice broke in a sob.

Arabella Kennedy straightened. "Don't trouble your head. *I* will handle the Lady Ana! We will put her in your old room as it has a good view of the garden."

"You mean Mother is to stay *here*?"

Cousin Bella's laugh was undoubtedly a major accomplishment. "Of course," she said practically, "she's family!"

Courtney was too overcome to reply. A pause. And then—

Cousin Bella cleared her throat significantly. "You are no longer a little girl, Courtney. You are Clint's wife!"

"Cousin Bella—please—I can't talk about that—"

Cousin Bella rang for tea. "You don't have to talk—just listen! We have all suffered, even gone to pieces at times. But you are pure Glamora. You have conquered your hurts because with that blood in your veins you have pulled yourself together and got on with your life in this new country. You are caught in love's trap. The New Woman the Lord and Clint have made of you will see you through. Remember, no longer a child . . ."

No longer a child. She must put away childish things.

Feeling a chill in spite of the warm day, Courtney pressed the warm teacup to her forehead. For a moment, she saw a small girl in a twisted-rope swing on the board her father had placed there. She was swinging . . . swinging . . . her dark hair first dragging the grass as she swung backwards in time, then her long skirts billowing out like a cloud as she swung forward. And then the vision faded, leaving Courtney to wonder as to the child's identity. Her? Or the child that had never been.

Cousin Bella was still talking. "You must remember, my dear, sweet Courtney, that you are never alone. You have all of us. And we have the Lord. We all share in this pain. We love you and we stand ready to make a new start. But Clint hurts, too. You must help him come to grips with that before he leaves—"

"Leave! Clint—*leave*?"

The words cut through her heart. Clint was going away. And he had not told her. But how long had it been since they had been alone together? Courtney set her china teacup aside, inhaling the scent of roses that blew in from Donolar's garden. She felt faint. Almost to the comatose state. Quietly she started to cry. The tears began to wash away the wall, leaving her defenseless but no longer angry. No longer guilty. There would be other children. But never another Clint.

Cousin Bella was talking again. Or maybe she had never stopped. "We are sending larger shipments from the mines and, unfortunately, the robbers never rest! Clint will accompany some of the silver to Puget Sound, stay until the shipments are bound down the Oregon coast—maybe go along a way—"

Somehow Courtney escaped, feeling a need to reexamine the lines of ancestors. She guessed they had hung there for so long that she hardly felt their presence anymore, like the love she had sublimated. But they were important—her bloodline—her *courage*. She paused to gather an impression of light curls and dark mustaches, of dated uniforms and stiff collars that stretched necks up to meet the world head-on. Her forebears, begging her to toughen up. Not take the easy way out. Courtney nodded as if to gain their approval.

"I have done my homework, gentlemen," Courtney smiled and imagined that they smiled back.

*　*　*

Somehow Courtney knew that Clint would come home the evening she and Cousin Bella talked. She dressed with care, after a leisurely lavender-scented bath. Well before the dinner hour, she heard Clint's deep, rich voice in conversation with his aunt. They were in the library.

Should she join them? No, it was best to go to the sun room. Once there, she was surprised to hear their voices float down.

"Mrs. Rueben is packing your clothes, Clint. But you must *not* leave before seeing Courtney . . . we have talked . . . ready for a reconciliation—"

"Reconciliation? We have had no differences."

"Would that you had! Sometimes a storm clears the air—"

Clint groaned. "Things change, Aunt Bella—relationships—*everything*."

"You can't tell me, Clint Desmond, that your love for your wife has changed—and she *is* your wife, you know—"

"I need no reminding, Aunt Bella, but you must let Courtney decide what she wants."

There was a hint of anger in Arabella Kennedy's voice when she answered. "She saw you through your blindness!"

"That was different. My loss. Loss of the unborn child belonged to us both. Let us handle it."

"But you aren't handling it—not at all!"

The musical sound of chimes sounded down the hall. The air was fragrant with pine and roses—red, Courtney felt sure, red for love. Time to make her presence known. Time to make all things right. How? God would have to guide her.

Mandy was placing the chimney on the lamp. Courtney stepped within the radius of light. Clint glanced at her and, obviously caught off-guard, his eyes sparkled as blue waters sparkle in the sunlight. He would rush to her and she would fall into his arms. There would be no need for talk . . .

But something had gone wrong. "How are you, Courtney?"

"Fine." The word choked in her throat. She stood very still, pulse clamoring. Surely he would unbend. She willed him to take the first step . . . give her another chance . . .

"We will talk when I return, Courtney. Please take care." Clint turned on his heel and was gone. Gone without a kiss . . .

CHAPTER 34
Thinking Backwards

Courtney was left numb. Cousin Bella wisely ordered supper sent up to her but seemed to know that this was no time to talk. Mandy, her great irises rolling like black marbles in saucers of milk, brought the tray.

"I do declare, Miz Desmond—Courtney, hon—it dun seems lonesum a'ready without Mistah Clint. But he be comin' back. Now, y'all be takin' care uv yoresef—"

Courtney nodded, unable to speak. She was exhausted. And nothing mattered. Nothing at all.

She began thinking backwards. Remembering her meeting with Clint on the train West. It had been more than attraction for them both. It was a once-in-a-life-time kind of love. Clint had taught her all over how to live . . . how to forgive the past . . . rally from her mistakes. And where had his teaching led? To the splendor of a dream too beautiful to endure. She had leaned upon his strength and tenderness and together they had spun a dream-child. But the tie she had thought so secure was impermanent, shifting like the morning sun in the tree-tops; frail as a silken cobweb. Oh, the ache of it all!

Courtney knelt by the window and tried to pray. But she found her mind wandering. Watching the road. Hoping that Clint would change his mind and return. But the sun slipped below the horizon, leaving a burst of iridescent splendor, gilt clouds lined with twilight's red-gold. Finally, the tallest trees caught the faint reflection of hyacinth, heralding the end of day. Earth and sky mellowed. But her heart was more fragile than the sliver of moon that lingered but a moment. And, like silken threads of love that once entwined two hearts into one, was gone . . .

*   *   *

That night Courtney dreamed of being on a train. As the wheels clanged steel-on-steel, clicked, and banged, Clint came to sit beside her. But before she could touch him, he had faded into the past. Lance came to console her. Then he, too, disappeared. The train huffed and puffed, rattled and rumbled to the accompaniment of her troubled thoughts. But what was this? Courtney herself disappeared. And Mother sat in her place. "Why are you taking me there, Efraim? Can't my children *ever* make an effort to consider their mother's needs? Vanessa marrying a commoner . . . Courtney stooping to wed a *miner* . . . and you, my trusted son, taking me to meet that deranged boy . . . what did you say his name was?"

And then the Bellevues appeared. Mother seemed satisfied.

Courtney was relieved when she awoke with a start. Little did she guess that the dream was only a faint foretaste of the future.

CHAPTER 35
Without Incident

Reconstruction began at Rambling Gate. Supply wagons rumbled by the Mansion. But Roberta, doubly busy during Efraim's absence, was never along. There was no chance for Courtney to prepare her for the Lady Ana. She found herself unable to prepare Donolar. So how would it be possible to prepare Roberta for an outsider? *Outsider*. What a bloodless word. Courtney was surprised at application of such language to her mother when Courtney had grown up feeling that the word described herself. Maybe all that was past.

The day Mother arrived, Courtney found herself on edge. Frightened. Unsure as to her role. It was not until afterwards that she recalled a pewter bowl on the table in the foyer. The bowl held only two long-stemmed roses. One was white, the other red. A delicate symbol of unity. Donolar's offering of love. Dear, sweet Donolar, whose love—like her own—had been rejected.

"The trip was without incident," Efraim said as he supported Ana Bellevue Glamora Ambrose once he had lifted her from the VanKotens' coach which he had borrowed. "Mother dear, here are your children."

"Mother!"

Courtney sprang forward. Once again a little girl begging to be loved. Once again captivated by the Dresden beauty of the woman before her. Mother's tapering hands, the only quality of Courtney's Bellevue legacy, fluttered helplessly.

Courtney never remembered if her mother returned her embrace. She was too conscious of Donolar clinging to her skirts as Efraim, assisted by Mandy, all but carried the Lady Ana upstairs. Mrs. Rueben had prepared Courtney's old room for Mother's first night. Later, she would move into the tower if that were her wish, Cousin Bella said.

"Can't we have the shutters open?" Mother's whispery voice pleaded. "It looks so dismal—"

"Hello, Ana!" Cousin Bella, who had followed without a word, cut Mother off in mid-sentence. "We will open the drapes at once. We do not want you to find life dismal here."

Ana Ambrose sank wearily onto the freshly made bed as Mandy opened the shutters to let in a flood of sunlight. Closing her eyes against the light (or was it life?), Mother said the trip had been awful . . . simply awful . . . and if they would all go away, she would like to rest.

Mrs. Rueben entered noiselessly. She would hang the guest's clothing in the closet, she said in broken English.

"Leave them as they are!" The voice, although soft, was a command. "I shan't be staying—and I have had no new gown for so long. Oh, life has been cruel . . . so cruel. Leave my trunks packed. And hurry my tea!"

"In due time, my dear Ana," Cousin Bella answered, her lips set in a straight, firm line. "And let us understand each other. You are welcome here for as long as you wish—but we do not order those in our employ around."

Mother dabbed at her eyes with a lace handkerchief. "Efraim, I told you I should bring my own servant—"

"We do not have *servants* at the Mansion, Ana. They are family. I hope you can grow accustomed to our ways."

Mother dabbed at her eyes again. Why must others scold her? "I must rest."

There was a soft whimper behind Courtney. Donolar!

Something inside Courtney snapped. "You may rest in a moment, Mother. We will care for your needs. But first, you will want to see Donolar."

Courtney stepped aside to show Donolar's beautifully childish face. But the Lady Ana did not open her eyes. "Not now, Courtney. Please do not be tiresome—"

Donolar turned and tiptoed down the stairs. The others followed. And the pattern was set.

The trip West had been without incident, Efraim had said. Courtney sighed and looked at Efraim with sad, dark eyes. She had expected to be overwhelmed. The opposite was true. Was there such as word as *under*-whelmed? She wondered what the future held for them all.

Downstairs, Courtney cried in her brother's arms. "What do you think? What can I do? I—I feel so helpless. And my whole world has fallen apart. Roberta will tell you—"

Efraim held her close. "We will work something out, little sister . . . I promise."

CHAPTER 36
A Period of Adjustment

In a heartbreaking sort of way, Mother's presence at the Mansion helped Courtney bear the agony of separation from Clint. It was no surprise that Ana Ambrose made no effort to adjust to her new surroundings. But Courtney had hoped—even sent many a prayer winging heavenward—that perhaps they would be able to talk. Her efforts to draw Mother out were in vain. And yet, trying as she did to meet the demands imposed upon her kept her sane. Only at night, often dozing at her mother's bedside until she was sure sleep came to the troubled woman, did Courtney's marriage occupy her mind to the exclusion of all else.

Oh, Clint, Clint, my darling, come home safely, her heart cried out. *I will make it all up to you, for the Lord has laid it upon my heart that the wall between us is of my own building.*

Courtney prayed then, unaware that she was giving voice to the words. "Forgive me, Lord . . . bring my husband back safely so that we can build the kind Christian family You intend as a fulfillment to love."

Mother moved restlessly. "What are you mumbling about, Courtney?"

"I am sorry to have disturbed you, Mother. I was praying."

Perhaps that was enough to say at the moment. But to Courtney's surprise, it was her mother who pursued the subject.

"Oh, you poor children. I fear I have failed you . . . but it was not my fault . . . life has been unkind. I never expected, however, that you and Efraim would engage in some kind of cult—"

Courtney gasped. "Oh, Mother, our faith is no cult! It—"

"Please do not interrupt!" Mother's voice sounded stronger. "I saw that foolish fish on Efraim's business card."

"You can be proud that he has the courage. The fish-shaped logo symbolizes Christian faith and each time Efraim hands a card to a client, he is spreading God's word."

Mother inhaled deeply as if in despair. Could she be overtired? Had Courtney said too much? It was her duty to honor her mother. "Are you all right, Mother?"

"Of course I am not all right—but stay." The voice had weakened. "Were your prayers for me?"

"No," Courtney admitted guiltily. "They were for Clint—"

"You have not brought this miner-husband to my bed-side." The weak voice carried an accusation. An accusation Courtney felt compelled to correct.

"Clint is away, Mother—"

And then, before she realized it, Courtney was telling of Clint's fine qualities, his gentleness with her, his love for Cousin Bella, Donolar, and the "family" (describing each member). Oh, that Mother could be strong enough to dine with them all soon. Clint was away now, but when he returned—

"If this man is so wonderful, why do you look so unhappy, so worn? He has abandoned you here in the wilderness, has he not? Left you as—" Ana Ambrose began to weep.

Courtney knelt beside the bed. "No, Mother—no, he would never do that. I—I—Clint and I were preparing to present you with a grandchild. I miscarried—"

Courtney burst into tears at the word. Her mother tried to soothe her with words that cut her heart out.

"Ah, my poor baby, how fortunate for you. Can't you see how ghastly it would be trying to bring a child into this kind of wilderness? You have been spared. Now, let us speak no more of such unpleasant things."

Courtney wiped away her tears and straightened her mother's covers. Something had happened. Something sad. But wonderful. Over and over, she had asked the Lord for guidance. But she had failed to look for (or perhaps it was to recognize) the solutions God provided. Now, He had shown her that there could be no loving relationship between herself and her mother. No longer would she drag the anchor of her past behind her!

CHAPTER 37
A Shocking Move

Day after day the Lady Ana refused to leave her room. She also refused to receive "guests." However, between them, Courtney and Cousin Bella saw to it that Brother Jim and Doc George entered the room.

Brother Jim stayed only a few minutes. What was there to say to a woman who first ignored him, then found fault with the land and its people without making their acquaintance? He would pray for her, he told Courtney. God knew how to deal with the octopus-like tentacles that squeezed out the life-giving blood that allowed her to love.

Four weeks passed before Cousin Bella brought Doc George to pay a call. The doctor and Cousin Bella had been behaving strangely of late, Courtney noted. As if they were holding back some secret that they were bursting to share but were determined to keep. Could it have to do with Mother? Courtney wished that whatever it was could add just a wee bit of Cousin Bella's sudden bloom to Mother.

Mother looked genuinely surprised when Doc George appeared with his black satchel. "Dr. George Washington Lovelace, doctor of homeopathic medicine, at your service, my beautiful lady."

"I sent for no doctor," Ana said civilly but with no welcome in her voice. "But I must say you look more like St. Nick."

The doctor laughed heartily. "At least you didn't say 'Old Nick,' the devil himself, Ma'm."

He was still chuckling when he felt for her pulse. "I can see that you doubt my credentials, but let me assure you that I do not practice in bloodletting or the use of boring holes in the skulls to allow the devils to escape—not even in counterirritation, peeling away live flesh . . ."

Mother shuddered. But before she was able to order her caller away, he had finished counting beats of the pale-blue vein on her frail wrist.

To Courtney's surprise, her mother began telling him about her vague complaints and imaginary illnesses. Courtney admired the way Doc George kept nodding his cloud of white hair and appeared all sympathy. Which meant he was preparing to deliver an unwelcome prescription.

"I understand—um-hmmm—I see—yes, yes. Now, what you need is some fresh country air. Begin with a short walk. Let Courtney show you the garden. Then the woods are lovely now—the leaves are turning. By the way, your daughter is a wonderful nurse. I predict that you will be well much sooner than you think. You see, I have a very special medicine I have saved just for you!"

"Surely you must be suffering from an acute attack of brain shock, Courtney! You never used to be so bold—bringing me a pugilist and then a quack," Mother sighed afterwards.

Nevertheless, she allowed herself to be helped to the end of the hall that evening to view an early-autumn sunset. Below—in carefully laid-out rows—were the last of the dahlias, which seemed to pick up the colors of the sunset, and the first of the approaching fall's chrysanthemums, some as pure as snowdrift, others as golden as freshly mined nuggets.

"The others are wildflowers. Some of them bloom the year round—thanks to Donolar's planning," Courtney said with pride.

But Mother was not listening.

Courtney was discouraged but determined. Mother must be coaxed outside.

When Roberta made an unexpected call, Courtney had a sudden idea. "Mother," she said, "may I present the daughter of Efraim's partner? Her father is restoring a beautiful old home farther up the way—"

"I am Roberta VanKoten," Roberta smiled, as she extended her well-groomed hand slipped from a doeskin glove and took Ana's limp hand in her own.

Courtney was embarrassed that in her eagerness to interest her mother, she had made an incomplete introduction. At the same time, it pleased her that Roberta—so completely changed in appearance and personality— had saved a bad moment.

"Your children's descriptions do not do you justice, Mrs. Ambrose, beautiful though they were."

Ana Ambrose scrutinized Roberta's smart tweed suit with an appreciative eye. But her health would not allow her to accompany the girls, she said—sounding almost sad.

Courtney had been confined far too long. Surely it would do Mother no harm to be alone while she walked with Roberta. She was glad she went. Rambling Gate was a revelation.

"I do wish Efraim could see the changes," Roberta said as she unlocked the door, "but he has been so busy since his return. He is plagued by guilt, too—your being left to care for your mother and the loss of—oh, Courtney, forgive me, but he was looking forward so much to being an uncle!"

"He will be!" Courtney promised rashly.

"Good girl! And your brother will be with you soon."

Courtney hoped so. There was so much to say. But for now, all questions could wait. She was thrilled at the scene before her. Roberta had done wonders.

A blazing log created shadows that danced from the calf-bound books on shelves lining either side of the fireplace, then lighted Lance's paintings above the mantel. Crimson roses filled the room with fragrance.

"Who—what—?" Courtney asked amazed.

"Donolar came ahead of us," Roberta laughed. "He wanted to surprise you. From here he went in search of goldenrod for your mother."

Courtney failed to hear Roberta's last statement, so engrossed was she in the enormous chairs, covered in red velvet to match the heavy drapes. Cara had done a beautiful job. Courtney's heart was filled with joy for she knew that Roberta would reward the Laughtens handsomely.

Roberta pulled aside a drape from the long window to show the beginnings of the court. One day the square tower would have its lacy iron balcony restored. Now it was near-hidden by blackberry vines that struggled to cover the main house. Then Courtney and Roberta ascended the stairway, already repaired and given back its lacelike balustrade, to explore the bedrooms where restoration was in progress.

"Wouldn't this be an enchanting place for a honeymoon?" There was a hint of a dream in Roberta's voice, causing Courtney's heart to quicken. But before she could speak there was the softly urgent call of a quail.

"Donolar!" Courtney bounded down the stairs without further words, sensing that something was amiss.

Donolar was breathless. Something had happened, he said. Something awful. *Horrible*-awful. She never had liked him. And now she was displeased. *She—*

"Who, darling? Who is *she*?"

And then Courtney's heart sank. Mother, he meant. What could have happened? But there was no way of asking more of Donolar. He was babbling foolishly and running like a helpless fox pursued by hunters. He was still running when he crossed the gardens of the Mansion, taking no note that they were kindled with the kiss of autumn's fire, seeking refuge in his Isle of Innisfree.

Mandy met Courtney at the door. Never before had Courtney seen her so angry—not even at Mrs. Rueben. "What h-happened?" Courtney asked breathlessly.

Mandy pulled herself as straight as a Washington fir tree. With pure-blooded African ire, she spoke: "Dat woman—I dun means de Lady Ana—she dun went 'n moved yore clothes from Mistah Clint's room. Ah means she made me 'n Miz Rueben move 'em fo' her—sayin' she'd see dat we wuz outta a job less'n we obeyed. She's tough, if y'all won' be mad at mah sayin' so—meaner'n Donolar's buttahflies when dey's vicious lak he sez. She dun busted some vases—eben de one what wuz holdin' de goldenrod 'cuz it made her sneeze. Dat made dat po' baby Donolar cry 'is heart out—'n dat ain't all—"

Courtney was seized by an all-consuming sense of frustration which rapidly turned to anger. "Cousin Bella did not order this move?"

"She dun gone wid Doc George Washington ridin'—oh, she gonna be mad. But, Courtney, hon, dat ain't all—wait! She throwed yore journal on de floah—den she fainted-like."

Courtney rushed into the bedroom. Her mother, looking like a beautiful ghost, lay across the bed. What was there to do but bathe her face—coax her back to life—?

"I've fallen overboard, Lord. The ocean is swallowing me up. I am helpless . . . marooned . . . and Clint is not here to rescue me . . . help me . . . *please* . . .

CHAPTER 38
A Letter at Last

After Mother's outburst she was as docile as a lamb. Courtney resigned herself to the situation but made up her mind that it was only temporary as Cousin Bella advised.

To Courtney's dismay, Arabella Kennedy shrugged off the tirade of her late cousin's wife as "typical." But (and again that secretive smile) her days as ruler of this household were numbered.

Efraim came and went. But there was little occasion for Courtney to have a word alone with him since Mother demanded most of his time.

In one of their brief conversations, Courtney asked her brother how it would all end. "You have your life—"

"Yes, darling, I do," he said. Did she only imagine the special shine of his eyes? "And so do you. I never did know exactly what went wrong between you and Clint—"

"I wish I could tell you, Efraim. It—it just happened. I am afraid I turned inward when I lost the baby—"

Efraim took her in his arms. "I am sorry that I was away—and have allowed business to keep me from helping here. You are a courageous little girl and I am proud of you. But you must make things right with your husband. You two are in love if ever I saw a couple in love."

"I am afraid I have driven him away. There has been no letter—"

"You know the mail, darling," Efraim said, stroking her hand. "Clint could hand deliver a letter faster than

177

the trains. As to Mother, can you manage just a short while longer? Cousin Bella has something in mind."

Courtney nodded. But her mind was on Clint.

That afternoon Clint's first and only letter came. Courtney tripped over her skirt in her rush to get back upstairs and to the library where she could be alone. At the landing she stopped. Above the pounding of her heart, she had heard a definite moan. It was hard to tell the direction from which the sound came. But when it was repeated, Courtney realized that it had come from her mother's room.

"Mother, are you ill?" she asked at the door.

Mother was sobbing. "No—no—do not bring that unpleasant doctor here again. I am tormented by what I have learned about this dreadful place. We must escape before it has the same effect on us. Certainly, such things do not run through our veins. It is madness that comes from the environs. And to think that you, a Bellevue, would be so thoughtless! My humiliation is complete— my life is over—"

"Mother, whatever are you talking about—?"

Why finish the question? For suddenly Courtney knew. Mother had read in her journal the account of the criminal records of the Bellevues.

"With all my heart," she said, "I wish it were not true. However, Mother, I truly feel that it is time you dealt with reality. What these distant relatives have done is no reflection on you. Each of us is responsible to God for the sins we ourselves commit. And even those He will forgive—"

"Are you going to preach to me? Have you turned against me and plan to punish me?" Mother's voice was pitifully low, a near-whisper—one of her best acts.

"Yes," Courtney said, with a lift of her chin. "Yes, I guess I am going to preach. I have not turned against you. I never will. You are my mother. And punish you? Only

God has that right. But, Mother, He would rather love you—"

"Don't speak to me of love!"

And then a miracle happened. There was a knock and Cousin Bella, without waiting for an invitation, walked in.

"You have a guest, Ana. This is your Cousin Horace. You Bellevues will find much to talk about, I am sure. And you, Courtney, may excuse yourself and read your mail."

The voice held a command and Courtney was propelled from the bedroom too suddenly to protest—had she planned to.

"Don't look so concerned, my dear," Arabella Kennedy said with a faint smile. "The two will get along famously. You see, her Cousin Bellevue will restore your mother's self-image, give her back pride in that blue-blooded name, and prepare her for what lies ahead."

Courtney was speechless, so Cousin Bella continued: "You have heard us speak often of Bellevue, Washington. The name came from the original family which came here about the time my ancestors came, so one story goes." She shook her head, adjusted a tortoiseshell comb, and went on, "There are people like Ana, you know— making false gods of background. But let us not deal with them harshly. There are gentler ways."

There was a look of cunning in the older woman's eyes. "I told you that I would deal with the Lady Ana. Leave the problem to me."

"I'm afraid I do not understand."

"You are not supposed to—yet."

Cousin Bella walked down the hall and descended the stairs. A confused Courtney stood still a moment, somehow recognizing that this was the beginning of Cousin Bella's plan.

And then she hurried into the library to read her husband's letter. Where was the letter opener anyway?

Impatiently, Courtney slit the envelope with a forefinger, unaware that she had slit her finger as well.

Quickly, she scanned the single sheet. Clint was well. The sales had gone well. He hoped she was well. *Well, well, well!* A word Doc George used on his patients. But the letter was signed, *Love, Clint*. Love, he had said, *love*. She must be satisfied with that.

CHAPTER 39
Ill-timed Return

Three days later Cousin Bella summoned Courtney to the sun room. The set of Cousin Bella's mouth spelled determination, but the same twinkle Courtney had noted in past weeks was present.

"Your mother," Cousin Bella said over tea, "is making a slow recovery at best."

Courtney stirred her tea. "I know," she said, looking sadly at the amber liquid, "but I have no idea what to do."

"*I* do. Ana has refused our every invitation to leave that room, so I plan to bring the world to her!"

"How do you propose to do that?"

"I plan a small dinner party—*very* small, and she is to be the guest of honor. In fact, there will be only the family—would that Clint were here, but we will carry on. Oh, there *will* be two guests, Efraim's partner and his daughter."

"I fail to see—" Courtney began doubtfully.

"Take a walk and think it over while I go up to invite your mother. Your job will be to do for her what you did for Roberta—make her lovely—choose a blue gown. That is her color—"

Courtney walked briskly through the autumn woods, inhaling deeply the wine-scents of overripe apples and the rooty smell of decaying gardens. Autumn, the dying of the year, was a time for reflection. But it was not upon her mother's plight that Courtney reflected. It was Clint.

"Lord, bring my mother peace. She is deeply troubled —but, forgive me, Lord, so am I. Whatever it is that Cousin Bella has in mind, please, I beg, let it work. For I need to be with my husband. Mother will not let go—and the idea frightens me. I know that You can bring Clint and me back together . . . oh, dear God, I love him so deeply . . ."

So deep was Courtney in her conversational prayer that she lost all count of time. It must be past noon. Reluctantly, she turned and retraced her steps toward the Mansion, savoring the heady perfume of the pines and balsams the sun coaxed from their fragrant needles. A strange peace stole into her heart. Nothing was settled. Miracles took time. But God, with a helper like Cousin Bella, just might hasten this one along.

Ana Ambrose's face looked unnaturally bright. "Arabella feels that a party would be in order."

"Oh Mother, so do I!" Courtney said excitedly. "I only wish Clint could join us—"

Mother's face clouded. "Clint Desmond was here and was polite once he overcame his agitation of your having moved—"

Clint! *Here?* What could he have thought except that she had moved out of his life?

"Courtney! What shall I wear?" Ana Ambrose spoke with impatience.

CHAPTER 40
Misunderstanding

On the day of the party, Courtney awakened early with such an overwhelming desire to see Clint that it was an ache that began in her chest and spread throughout her body. Mother was still sleeping, so she slipped out of bed. Even as she thrust her arms through the sleeves of a light robe, Courtney had no plan in mind. In the hall, however, she was drawn by an invisible magnet to the door of the room she had shared with Clint.

She would never know why she knocked. The room was unoccupied.

Only it wasn't! Without waiting for a response, Courtney turned the knob and entered. She was greeted by the dearly familiar smell. Bay rum. Wool. And something intangibly masculine that said Clint. It was too much to bear. Courtney let out a small cry and would have fled had there not been firm footsteps behind her.

"Mrs. Clinton Desmond, unless I am mistaken!"

It had to be a dream. The same dream she had dreamed over and over. Courtney had imagined seeing Clint again—but never like this! His hair was tousled and he was slipping one long arm into a robe somewhat clumsily and reaching for her with the other.

"Clint—Clint, you're home—" she murmured foolishly. It was still a dream in spite of the low, rich laugh.

But Courtney knew it was real when Clint pulled her closer, closer, *closer*.

"There's been a terrible mistake, Clint—I—we—"

Clint drew back. Even in the half-light of early dawn, she could see the blue, blue eyes that pierced her soul. *Oh darling, darling, forgive me,* Courtney wanted to cry out. But the dream was back—the kind of dream that robs one of speech, renders one unable to move. And so she did not return her husband's embrace.

And then the moment, like the dream she had imagined, was gone. There was a pounding on the door, followed by Horace Bellevue's frantic voice.

"The *arrasta*—Clint, do you hear me? *Clint!*"

Courtney's legs would no longer support her. She dropped into Clint's wing-back chair. Maybe they talked. She never could remember what they said if they did. Yes, they must have, for she remembered later that Clint said he would be unable to join them this evening. And he would be at the mines if she needed him. *If she needed him.* She needed him *now.* He had misunderstood.

But Clint was gone.

CHAPTER 41
Love at Second Sight

The ache was still with Courtney as she dressed her mother's hair for the evening. The blue gown accentuated her delicate skin and brought added sheen to the golden tresses.

"I do look as if I could enter fashionable society instead of—"

"You look lovely, Mother."

"I wish you could have inherited the Bellevue beauty like Vanessa," Mother sighed. "But with the right clothes —Courtney, I do wish you had married Lance."

"I am not in love with Lance," Courtney said tiredly.

"Bah," Ana Ambrose scoffed, patting a curl. "So your husband pointed out, but I—"

"You and Clint talked about—me?" Courtney dropped the hairbrush.

Mother shrugged as if it were unimportant. And then she said vaguely, "I was supposed to give you some silly message—let me think, oh yes, you were to meet him in his room that night—"

"*Our* room," Courtney corrected. "Oh, Mother, do you realize what you have done?"

* * *

Robert VanKoten looked impressive, carrying an ivory-tipped cane and holding gray dinner gloves which matched his silk vest. He bowed and extended a well-groomed hand to the honored guest.

"Ah, my dear Lady Ambrose, how charming you are, my dear."

Mother's eyes sparkled and she blushed in the most feminine sort of way. Her fragility carried a plea for protection. It was easy to see that Mr. VanKoten was carried away. It was easy to see, also, that Cousin Bella's party was a complete success—more aptly, a triumph!

Cousin Bella seated the two of them together, of course. The others took their usual places except that Roberta occupied the chair left vacant by Clint's absence which, conveniently, was beside Efraim.

Certainly everyone had gone all out for the evening. Donolar had created a magnificent centerpiece of golden mums and maidenhair fern. On either side of the centerpiece, Cousin Bella's ancient silver candlesticks held candles whose flames rivaled the chrysanthemums' glowing color. And, in the mirrors, Mother's beautiful reflection repeated over and over for the admiring eyes of Roberta's father.

Unusually festive as the atmosphere was, Arabella Kennedy made no change in the routine. Mandy read the Scripture. Brother Jim prayed, mentioning everyone present, and everyone said, "Amen."

Throughout dinner Ana Ambrose and Robert Van-Koten had eyes only for each other. Mother, Courtney noted, was all innocence. Flattered by it, Mr. VanKoten explained numerous matters in which Courtney had never known her mother to show an interest. The others, seemingly inspired by the attraction between the two, talked and laughed among themselves.

Mother tensed only one time. And that was short-lived. The incident occurred when Mother overheard Courtney telling Efraim that Horace Bellevue had come for Clint. Too late, she realized that Mother—while impressed by Horace—was reluctant to have Mr. VanKoten know of the brothers who had put a blight on the family name.

Ana Bellevue Ambrose covered beautifully. Looking helplessly at her new acquaintance, she said, "Horace tells me that a city here on the frontier bears our name."

"Ah yes, my dear Ana," Robert VanKoten hastened to respond. "And you, having traveled in Europe, may be aware of the beautiful neighborhood of Bellevue outside Paris—undoubtedly the home of your ancestors."

Mother's eyes begged for more.

"Formerly a palace, it overlooks the valley of the Seine . . . built in the 1700's . . . embellished by French artists . . . most charming residence in all Europe . . . sold after the Revolution, but retains the famous name . . ."

"Oh," Mother breathed, "I would love to see it."

"And someday perhaps you will—"

Their voices dropped in private conversation. When Mandy brought apple cobbler with her special fluffy spice sauce, Mr. VanKoten praised her profusely and then asked if he and the Lady Ambrose could be excused. A little walk would do them good. It was Doc George who agreed heartily.

For a moment after their departure, all was silent in the great dining room except for their receding footsteps. Each seemed buried in a private memory of starry skies over the green gloom of the dark forest.

It was Cousin Bella who spoke first. "I predict that we will be receiving handsomely engraved announcements one of these days: 'Mr. Robert VanKoten is proud to announce that the Lady Ambrose has consented to become his wife'!"

"So soon?" Roberta answered her hostess, but her eyes were on Efraim. "Love at first sight?"

"Second sight," Cousin Bella said knowingly. "Your father had a glimpse of the lady the day she arrived."

Further conversation was prevented by footsteps. The night had grown chill, Mr. VanKoten said with concern in his voice. And Ana Ambrose, with excitement in hers, said that Mr. VanKoten Esquire felt that she would be happier in the city. Perhaps she should move in—to be near Efraim.

CHAPTER 42
Proposal

The world was vibrant with color. A blue veil of wood smoke hovered over the settlement. Appropriate color, Cousin Bella said. The "something blue" for the Thanksgiving weddings, she added with the hint of a dream in her voice.

"Have you heard from Clint?" she asked after a pause.

Courtney shook her head. "Maybe there will be no response to my—my letter. I have treated him shabbily, but if he will accept my—my invitation—"

Arabella Kennedy's eyes still carried that knowing shine. "He will! Lots of surprises will be taking place. I wonder just how many weddings there will be . . ."

How many weddings?

Courtney's thoughts turned backward to Mother's sudden departure. Was that only a week ago? Already it seemed like a dream—undoubtedly because of the whirl of events. Cousin Bella's plan had worked. The Lady Ana, even in this "wilderness," was with her "own kind." What the future held for her time would tell; but, for the present, Courtney's mind was occupied 24 hours a day with what the future held for her and Clint. God had answered so many of her prayers that He would not let the most important one of all go unanswered. He would provide a way. And whatever path He revealed to her, Courtney Glamora Desmond would follow.

His answer came in such an unexpected way that Courtney smiled and imagined that the Lord smiled with her. It was Brother Jim who served as His mouthpiece.

"You know, I've given a lot of thinking to the Thanksgiving service. Seems to me that the mate for whom a man forsakes all others is his greatest gift. How can things be well in the church if they are not well at home? It would be a great testimonial if couples renewed their vows. We can call it a Day of Rededication—what do you think?"

His question hung in midair at dinner the night Mother had moved "to be near Efraim." Courtney looked around the table, wondering just why Brother Jim chose to ask the family before making mention to the congregation. After all, Doc George was a widower and all the others were unmarried (Brother Jim calling himself another "Paul")—all were unmarried, that is, except for herself and Clint. And could one call what they shared right now a marriage in the true sense?

And yet, to her surprise, Courtney felt herself speaking in words that could have been a foreign tongue. "I find the idea very timely. I will be as bold as a lion for righteousness."

The note she sent to Clint by Brother Jim was simple: "Meet me at the altar Thanksgiving Day. I want to be your wife!"

CHAPTER 43
Hasty Preparations

Women of the valley worked feverishly. Cara's sewing machine whirred around the clock. "More'n love has growed," she giggled to Courtney, ripping the hand-stitched gown of one lady whose middle had expanded with the passing of the years.

Courtney's dress needed no alterations. Her waist was as trim as the memorable day she had taken her wedding vows. But the garment must be aired and pressed. Her white, high-button shoes, unworn since the Christmas wedding, must be polished. And her hair, shining as always, must shine even more. Courtney was tempted to do it in an upsweep. The style would be perfect for the wreath of white roses Donolar planned to weave as a headpiece. But no, Clint used to like her hair cascading to her shoulders, just as he liked the simple center-part.

"Should I wear the veil?" Courtney pondered aloud in one of her rare moments with Cousin Bella.

"Oh, yes, yes indeed! But I *do* like the idea of the floral headpiece. I was hoping you would not use the seed pearls—"

Dear Cousin Bella. What an interest she was taking in the repeating of vows between husbands and wives of the congregation. It would strengthen the ties of the entire settlement, she said, and it must be "just right."

But Courtney suspected that the excitement sprang from something more. It would bring together the two young people who were as dear as her own children and

191

(Cousin Bella admitted slyly) extend the family . . . give her "grandchildren."

Courtney prayed fervently that the ceremony would do just that, and she dared not think otherwise. In order to dispel any possible doubts about Clint's appearance at the altar, Courtney thought about Cousin Bella's concentration on every detail, her eyes sparkling as if she had taken a dip in the Fountain of Perpetual Youth. Spurred by her high spirits, Mandy and Mrs. Rueben redoubled their efforts. The windows were washed, the furniture rubbed to a high gloss, and every leaf of the house plants wiped free of dust with castor oil from Doc George's black bag. Pound cakes, applesauce cakes, and green-tomato mincemeat pies were in the making. Enough for the army, they agreed, and neighbors would be bringing more—corn puddings, chowder, condiments, all the trimmings to enhance baked hams, wild turkeys, and stuffed grouse.

"All's gonna be awright if de men foks stay from undah-foot. Ah neber knowed Doctah George Washin'ton wuz t'be so much in mah kitchun. Uh body'd thank *he* wuz a'gonna take uh wife! Him 'n Miz Arabella'd be dyin' if de re-re—uh, *ception* wuz gonna be elsewheres!"

* * *

Efraim and Roberta dropped by the day before Thanksgiving. Roberta, looking radiant in a pine-green suit which brought out the jade spokes in her amber eyes, handed a package to Courtney.

"Here is the material you ordered for Cara Laughten. And I added a few buttons and bows on my own. How sweet of you to have thought of providing her with a dress for tomorrow."

"It took very little imagination," Courtney said humbly. "I asked if the neighbors kept her too busy to allow time for reviving her own wedding dress. She told me, without a hint of complaint, that she was married in a tattered calico skirt—none too clean—and an old shirt of her brother's, following a massacre on the Applegate Trail. I owe her so much—"

"Don't we all?" Roberta said warmly. "But we owe even more to you," she added with a significant glance. "Cara, incidentally, credits you with helping her work through her marital problem—helped her swallow her pride—"

"We all have to do that sometimes."

"Hey, you two! Stop talking in riddles," Efraim broke in. "Roberta wanted to make a final check of Rambling Gate. News of the big event has spread to the city and there is sure to be a big turnout of couples wishing to make a new commitment. Either these Westerners stay together for life as our Maker intended or (he smiled) a lot of them have begun to crack under the strain and look to Brother Jim to tend their wounds."

"It's a sacred step," Roberta said pensively, "marriage, I mean." Then, quickly, she shifted the subject. "In case the Mansion overflows, there's Rambling Gate—"

Roberta rode on alone. Efraim remained behind to chat with Courtney. He would join Roberta later, he promised.

"Horace wants to come—that would please Mother."

"Does that mean Mother's coming to church? Oh, Efraim!"

Efraim touched her cheek tenderly. "We have not come that far," he said with regret. "Give her time, darling. In fact, Mother is one of the subjects I wanted to discuss with you. Mr. VanKoten and I have a business trip scheduled for the day after Thanksgiving. We need to go to San Francisco. Roberta has persuaded Mother to go along. She is delighted with the prospect of shopping, seeing an opera—so she wishes to rest Thanksgiving—Roberta will go with us—"

"But you will be there to hear Clint and me renew our vows?" Courtney asked anxiously. "You and Roberta?"

"That was the other matter I wanted to talk about. You and Clint are going to—" Efraim paused awkwardly.

"Going to say 'I do' again? Of course, we are! Vows are too sacred to break. Ours bent a little—but they never broke. They never will!"

Then why was she crying as she turned away? "Oh, Efraim, please tell Horace we will expect him—Clint and I—"

"Dear God, dear God, let Clint meet me halfway," Courtney prayed as she stumbled up the stairs to lay out her wedding gown.

CHAPTER 44
"To God Be the Glory!"

"What a day!"

Courtney nodded wordlessly at Cousin Bella's greeting. There *were* no words for a day like this. Clear. Windless. Stinging cold. A perfect Thanksgiving, filled with anticipation such as the valley had never known before.

"Mandy and Mrs. Rueben will help you dress. Hurry, my dear—Donolar's waiting. He must be at the church early for the decorating and you will be with him—offering suggestions—and being well out of sight in case Clint wants to come home to dress—the groom must not see the bride, you know—"

It was uncharacteristic of Cousin Bella to talk so much and so rapidly. But it did not occur to Courtney that her cousin had an ulterior motive. She was incapable of thinking even after she and Donolar were on their way to the Church-in-the-Wildwood in a buggy overflowing with musk roses.

Donolar, too, talked endlessly. Did Courtney know that the Spaniards held Thanksgiving in Florida a century before the pilgrims and Indians stuffed their first turkey at Plymouth Rock? . . . Yes, Florida . . . 1565 . . . dining on garbanzo beans and salt pork laced with garlic . . . it all began with Ponce de León in "the Land of Flowers." Which reminded Donolar that he had saved his thornless roses for their Cousin Bella. Did Courtney know the thornless variety meant an early attachment that developed out of friendship?

Courtney sat stiffly beside her brother, hardly hearing his endless prattle about his conversations with "that Mr. VanKoten who knows so much." Donolar, too, was behaving strangely. It was unlike him to talk so much. But all of Courtney's bravado had faded. She was incapable of feeling anything at all except a hard, useless knot where her heart used to be. She was made of pottery. Pottery so brittle it would shatter at the touch of a hand.

What if Clint did not meet her?

Inside the church, the odor of roses was overpowering as Donolar arranged great baskets at the altar, set vases in the windows, and draped the crude, hand-hewn pews with festoons of buds nestled among golden-leafed vines of wild grapes, their clusters of purple fruit still intact.

One moment the church was empty except for the two of them. The next, it was overflowing. And Brother Jim, in an ancient suit, complete with tails that made him look like an overstuffed frog, was standing behind the bedecked altar. So hushed was the church that one could hear the whisper of the pines and the chatter of squirrels in search of one last nut.

"Is it well with thee?" Brother Jim bellowed.

Courtney was incapable of joining in any answering chorus there may have been. Neither was she capable of lifting her eyes to search for Clint. Maybe she was afraid of seeing that hurt look in the blue-lake eyes, the look of longing, the look of need. How could she have imagined that he did not share her grief? That she had nothing left to give? Why, she had everything, *everything*. And yet she had turned him away, responding politely to his words and rejecting his love.

Courtney came from her reverie with a start. What had Brother Jim said that caused the hordes of couples to go trooping to the altar? Then, blessedly, he repeated the invitation:

"With apologies to the gospel writers, Matthew, Mark, and Luke who wrote that 'the last shall be first,' I want to reverse the order with a special purpose! So, will all the 'firsts' come forward? All those who have been married 50 years or more—oh, we praise the Lord for you and share with you your reward of children and grandchildren! Now, those who've weathered life together for 35 years . . . 25 years . . ."

The countdown went on. The bright-eyed women, some in faded dresses that whispered of long-ago ceremonies and all carrying bouquets that trembled, faced their chosen mates, pink-cheeked and smiling. Why, there were multitudes!

"Bless you—bless you," Brother Jim kept saying emotionally. "Ten . . . five . . . four . . ."

On the count of *three*, Courtney panicked and would have bolted out the door had a firm, familiar hand not gripped her arm from behind. That touch! That wonderful, magical, tender touch. She knew it even before any words passed between them.

"Our count! One year with the only woman I will ever love—"

"Oh, Clint, *Clint*—"

Courtney whirled to face her husband, feeling a white rose petal drop from her crown and watching in fascination as it settled on the handkerchief of Clint's pocket. Right above his heart! And then she was in his arms.

Brother Jim cleared his throat. "*One!*" He repeated. "Will any couple reaching the first milestone come forward?"

With Courtney's veil askew and Clint's carefully folded handkerchief dabbing at his wife's eyes, the two approached the altar to join the others. Soon they would begin their vows. And then—oh, wonderful *then*—they would all celebrate Thanksgiving together and families would go their separate ways. All seemed to be of the same mind, having eyes only for one another. And that is how they missed the minister's last call:

" 'The last shall be first'—first to be honored, that is. Dearly beloved, if there be two of you among us wishing to enter the holy state of matrimony, push your way through this throng—*forthwith!*"

There was a swish of taffeta, then a childish motion from beside Brother Jim. Donolar! Donolar curling a finger of invitation and looking over the heads of the crowd while holding out the bouquet of thornless roses —*for Cousin Bella!*

Arabella Kennedy, an ivory taffeta-clad dowager-angel with black satin braids, accepted the roses, standing as straight and proud as a Douglas fir. Then she turned to meet the merrily twinkling eyes of Dr. George Washington Lovelace. For them the grandfather clock had turned backward. Life was at its beginning.

At its beginning. That was true of Courtney and Clint. It was true of all the other couples at the altar. And, as Brother Jim was saying, it was true of the Church which may have been "blown about like a straw in the wind but was finding its way back as the true "Bride of Christ, the living Savior . . . driving Satan to an early grave . . . the Lord, who had known all along that cream always rose to the top!"

It was all so wonderful—too wonderful to be absorbed. Courtney, still caught up in the dream-come-true, only half-heard Cousin Bella and Doc George exchange vows. The holy words seemed to fill the church for a lifetime as Brother Jim read from the Scriptures on and on. "Wives, submit yourselves unto your own husbands, as it is fit in the Lord. . . . Husbands, love your wives . . ."

And, yet, it must have taken only minutes, for the time had come for couples to renew their promises to God and their mates. "I, Courtney, love thee, Clint . . . and promise to remain ever your loving wife so long as we both shall live . . ."

Courtney's heart hammered as she joined in the words all wives (surely there must be a million!) were saying. It was when she dared lift her eyes to meet Clint's that it happened. There she read the love and tenderness of their wedding day multiplied tenfold. And, without warning, she burst into tears. Quietly at first, then in a sweeping tide that left her defenseless but ready to face life "from this day forward" with Clint at her side.

She cried for the child they had lost. But there would be others—12 of them! She cried for the years Cousin Bella and Doc George had lost, as well. But the shattered bones of those lost years would flesh out into something more beautiful—a starved relationship developing into a rich, mature love. She cried for all her mother had missed and for Brother Jim's "rebellious few still cater-wauling in the dark" who must be prayed back into the church. Finally, she cried for the surge of joy that comes when hearts awaken to love!

Courtney was in Clint's arms when she realized that all the tears were not hers! Clint was weeping too—openly and unashamedly, wiping away her tears and then his own as he held her against his heart. Cousin Bella wept, too—iron tears that came hard for a pioneer woman who had held her emotions imprisoned for so long.

And then everybody was weeping at once. Tears of repentance. For words spoken and words unspoken. But Brother Jim's prayers had been answered. His flock had come home for Thanksgiving. Like the underdog who had become world champion, the ex-prizefighter lifted his arms in victory:

To God be the glory—forever—amen!

* * *

Dinner was finished. Dishes were done. And the songs of praise were still. But the music lingered in Courtney's heart. There was so much to say. And no need to say it at all. Love's resourceful fingers would unknot all the contradictions. She and Clint would spend the rest of their lives keeping the vows to one another and to the Giver of all good things . . . loving without reservation . . . healing the broken spirit . . . feeding the hungry . . . building the valley with Christ as the Cornerstone . . . seeking the lost . . . and (she blushed) building a family!

The blush was not lost on her husband. "We are alone," he smiled. "Just us two with the Mansion all to ourselves."

It was true. Roberta had pressed the key to Rambling Gate into Doc George's palm when she and Efraim offered congratulations. As was the custom, the crowd had followed the newlyweds, while banging on pots and pans in the shivaree. And (wonder of wonders!) Mandy, shouting something about the "awful glory" of it all, had looped her arms through Mrs. Rueben's and dragged her along.

"So, do we walk off that dinner now or wait until you open your package?" Clint teased.

"Oh Clint, you remembered! And I have no groom's gift for you."

"It is for *us*. But if you want to walk first—"

"Oh darling, you know I can't wait!"

"I hoped you couldn't," Clint grinned as he pulled a large packing crate marked KENNEDY MINES COMPANY STORE from the hall closet where they had stood since seeing the wedding party off.

Moments later they were kneeling together as, with trembling fingers, Courtney peeled the final newspaper wrapping from the contents of the box. And then, with a cry of joy, she lifted stacks of tiny undershirts, fleecy flannel gowns, long dresses that, held high, reached from where she knelt to touch the floor, wee booties, and a baby-bunting complete with a hood. There was more, but Courtney was crying again and unable to go on with the unpacking because she had found the greatest treasure of all. Clint had pinned her note to a receiving blanket! Her proposal.

"Don't cry, sweetheart. I hoped you still wanted—"

"Oh, Clint, I do, I do!" Courtney's voice was muffled in Clint's handkerchief. "I just thought you had forgotten—"

With a little moan, Clint reached out and pulled her to him. There was pain in his voice when he spoke. "How could I forget? I was so afraid of losing you—and that would have been too much to bear after we lost the baby. So I eased the emptiness by having Cara, Aunt Bella, and Roberta help from the moment it—it happened—but why do we sit here drowning in tears? How about that walk so we can count our blessings, Mrs. Desmond?"

Mrs. Desmond took her husband's hand. Had she not promised to submit to his judgment?

Sunset had faded. The thin arms of late autumn twilight were too frail to hold back the darkness. But there was a sickle moon, protected by two brilliant guards, Venus and Jupiter, smiling down on the two loving hearts God Himself had awakened. A shooting star traversed the heavens to scatter stardust over the dark forest. And somewhere an owl hooted to its mate. Its sound was now friendly and mellow.

The air was thin and rare. As if the two of them stood high on a mountaintop. Alone. Together. Their only companion He who had known the end from the beginning.

Clint took Courtney's hands and warmed them between his own, then tucked them inside his jacket as they walked, silently counting the stars.

"One million one," Clint said at last of his blessings. "But," he paused to turn back toward the Mansion-in-the-Wild, "there await that many more. Come to think of it, I have never carried you across the threshold!"

Without waiting, he scooped her up, holding her close to his hammering heart. "My madonna—my darling madonna, my *wife!*"

Courtney was too overcome for words. She relaxed and listened as the music grew louder in her heart.

To God be the glory . . .
Forever . . .
Amen!

HARVEST HOUSE PUBLISHERS

For The Best In Inspirational Fiction

RUTH LIVINGSTON HILL CLASSICS

Bright Conquest
The Homecoming
The Jeweled Sword
Morning Is For Joy
This Side of Tomorrow
The South Wind Blew Softly

JUNE MASTERS BACHER
PIONEER ROMANCE NOVELS

Series 1

Love Is a Gentle Stranger
Love's Silent Song
Diary of a Loving Heart
Love Leads Home

Series 2

Journey to Love
Dreams Beyond Tomorrow
Seasons of Love
My Heart's Desire

Series 3

Love's Soft Whisper
Love's Beautiful Dream
When Hearts Awaken

MYSTERY/ROMANCE NOVELS

Echoes From the Past, *Bacher*
Mist Over Morro Bay, *Page/Fell*
Secret of the East Wind, *Page/Fell*
Storm Clouds Over Paradise, *Page/Fell*
Beyond the Windswept Sea, *Page/Fell*
The Legacy of Lillian Parker, *Holden*
The Compton Connection, *Holden*
The Caribbean Conspiracy, *Holden*

PIONEER ROMANCE NOVELS

Sweetbriar, *Wilbee*
The Sweetbriar Bride, *Wilbee*
The Tender Summer, *Johnson*

Available at
your local Christian bookstore

Dear Reader:

We would appreciate hearing from you regarding the June Masters Bacher Pioneer Romance Series. It will enable us to continue to give you the best in inspirational romance fiction.

Mail to: Pioneer Romance Editors
Harvest House Publishers, 1075 Arrowsmith
Eugene, OR 97402

1. What most influenced you to purchase **WHEN HEARTS AWAKEN**?
   - ☐ The Christian story
   - ☐ Cover
   - ☐ Backcover copy
   - ☐ _____
   - ☐ Recommendations
   - ☐ Other June Masters Bacher Pioneer Romances you've read

2. Where did you purchase **WHEN HEARTS AWAKEN**?
   - ☐ Christian bookstore
   - ☐ General bookstore
   - ☐ Other
   - ☐ Grocery store
   - ☐ Department store

3. Your overall rating of this book:
   - ☐ Excellent ☐ Very good ☐ Good ☐ Fair ☐ Poor

4. How many Bacher Pioneer Romances have you read altogether?
   (Choose one) ☐ 1-2 ☐ 3-6 ☐ 7-11 ☐ Over 11

5. How likely would you be to purchase other Bacher Pioneer Romances?
   - ☐ Very likely
   - ☐ Somewhat likely
   - ☐ Not very likely
   - ☐ Not at all

6. Please check the box next to your age group.
   - ☐ Under 18
   - ☐ 18-24
   - ☐ 25-34
   - ☐ 35-39
   - ☐ 40-54
   - ☐ Over 55

Name _____

Address _____

City _____ State _____ Zip _____